TWIN PLANETS

Earth and Firma were twin planets—mirror worlds on a single time-track. Now Firma was halted in its rotation around the sun by the Aliens. Unless Denning and Liston, twin humans, could destroy the Aliens and get Firma moving again, Earth would someday repeat Firma's tragedy and be burned to a cinder.

The Aliens had an incredible array of weapons at their disposal. Denning and Liston had only their courage and their brains.

TWIN PLANETS

PHILIP E. HIGH

LONDON
DENNIS DOBSON

First Published in Great Britain 1968
by DOBSON BOOKS LTD.,
80 Kensington Church Street, London W.8.

Reproduced and printed by
Latimer Trend & Co. Ltd., Whitstable

SBN 234 77281 6

Chapter One

Denning had not realized that the events of the past week had shaken him so much until his eyesight started playing tricks.

He *had* seen it, hadn't he? He stopped, put his car into reverse and went slowly backwards. It was an illusion, a trick of the light, surely?

It wasn't.

There was a small shelter containing a seat and a raised metal sign. The metal sign said *Stus Bop*.

He climbed out of the car and looked again. Clearly it was not a joke. The sign was weather-worn, and it was unlikely that the local authorities would permit such a glaring mistake to go unchanged for long. One knew, of course, that the sign meant "Bus Stop" but, even after rubbing one's eyes, it still said *Stus Bop*.

He frowned, irritated to find that the mistake had shaken him, and climbed back into the car. Better take a rest. If he were that shaken he'd better get off the road before he had an accident.

He pulled onto the grass verge, cut the engine and shivered. Damned cold, wasn't it? Strange, the sun had been shining only a few moments ago; now the sun had vanished and the sky had a curiously leaden sheen.

He shivered again. God, he *was* cold, really cold, but this was July, not January. Probably a fall in temperature due to an approaching storm, or more likely still, nerves, sheer nerves. The cold was nerves, the "bus stop" nerves, the whole business an aftermath of shock.

He lit a cigarette, made certain the handbrake was on

and closed his eyes. Better relax, try to sleep for a few moments. He'd be better after some rest.

In sleep Denning looked boyish, helpless and curiously ineffectual for his thirty years. He had good features: a strong chin, a well shaped mouth and awake, clear gray eyes beneath dark, rather thick brows. Nonetheless, he still looked guileless and vaguely apprehensive, as if he had been shut away from the world too long and was doubtful of its attitude towards him.

Perhaps the expression was indicative because Denning had discovered the previous week that he *was* guileless, *was* ineffective.

He had also discovered, to his chagrin, that he was a physical and moral coward. In truth, the only justification he could find for his continued existence was the fact that he could admit these things to himself without trying to justify them or explain them away.

He went over the events again. Yes, he was a coward. He should have hit Beacham, struck out at him however ineffectively, if only to justify his own manhood.

The trouble was, of course, that Beacham was bigger. The muscles in his naked shoulders had rippled unpleasantly, and he had looked crude, savage and too confident.

Beacham had stuck out his chin, almost demanding to be punched, and then he had sneered, "Don't burst into tears, sonny boy. These things happen and will probably happen again—or would you care to do something about it?"

It was then that Denning discovered he was a coward. He had retreated behind a torrent of clichés, a flood of deprecation. He heard the nauseatingly familiar phrases as if they were not his own. They were "civilized people," he had said. Then, "differences could be settled without violence." And so it went until the pathetic flood of words

6

slowly dried and he found himself near to tears and fumbling for a cigarette.

Beacham had laughed, laughed until the tears came into his eyes, and even Marian, who had not known whether to look guilty or brazen, had joined in shrilly, if a little hysterically.

Denning writhed inwardly. You came home unexpectedly because you had forgotten some necessary papers and found a business associate in bed with your wife. All you could do when they stood and laughed at you was to cringe, clenching and unclenching your hands ineffectually. But you knew suddenly that Marian, who was thirty-two, had married you for security. You knew that this was but one of many infidelities. You knew that this was not a love affair, but an incident. This act of adultery was as casual and as meaningless as a meal in a restaurant. God, and he had talked of "stepping aside for their future happiness." No wonder they had laughed.

He had wanted to hit Beacham, wanted to punch the thick sensuous lips until they were pulp; the resentment and the urge had been there, but his muscles had refused to respond.

Worse, he saw Beacham every day at work, and every day Beacham smirked and said, "Good morning, sonny boy."

It was clear also, by the sly looks of some of his colleagues and the embarrassed pity of others, that Beacham had related both his conquest and the subsequent "scene" to the entire staff.

Denning worked for a small firm of industrial architects and, for the last week, he had been using his entire will-power to go to work.

He was, he knew, a competent but uninspired architect with little hope of achieving sensational success, but at least he had been secure and almost content. Now he was a clown, a cuckold, despised by his associates and, no doubt, being reappraised by his employers.

At home, it was almost as bad. Marian was either out or shut in her room and, if they met, she called him "cave-worm."

Denning realized suddenly that he was bitterly cold and opened his eyes. It was clear that his nerves——

His mind froze with his body and became blank and uncomprehending. It couldn't be, *it couldn't*. Deep down inside him he whimpered.

There was no shelter, no bus stop, no familiar road, and a shrieking wind buffeted madly at the stationary car.

It was almost dark. Stars were visible and the sky was lit at the poles by an aurora such as had never been seen.

He blinked painfully. Ahead of him, a mile-wide road stretched to a horizon that looked like a burned black line against a white and crimson fire which flared like the open door of a blast furnace.

Denning put his hands over his eyes. "Hell," he thought, dully. "I'm dead. I must have been killed somewhere, probably in a road accident."

He looked again at the horizon, at the long black shadows leaning in darkness from every mound and hill, at the rim of fire encompassing the visible curvature of the Earth. It looked like a sunset gone mad.

Clearly, this was hell, but a Scandinavian hell of green ice and cold vipers——

Slowly his mind began to function and, by degrees, to reason. There was ice on the hood of the car, and the windshield was filigreed with frost. When you died, when you were killed, did you take your car with you? Would you be smoking the same cigarette? Somehow, none of it made sense and he was filled with an overwhelming panic. *Got to get away from here, got to turn the car around and head away from that ghastly burning glare.*

He fumbled, shaking for the switch and turned it sharply

to the right. The starter groaned, the engine turned protestingly, missed, faltered and finally fired unevenly. Vaguely he was glad he had not drained the antifreeze of the previous winter.

The first time he tried to pull away, the engine stalled and he had to restart, but the second time the engine had almost settled down to its familiar purr.

The opposite direction was, he found, no more encouraging than the flaring horizon from which he had turned. The distant heights which faced him might have been normal mountains, but he didn't think they were. The jagged peaks and long surfaces which threw back the glare almost like mirrors could mean only one thing—ice. Mountains of ice, enormous glaciers rising tier upon tier as far as he could see.

God, he was so cold. His feet felt numb and the middle finger of his right hand was white and bloodless.

He turned on the heater and was grateful for the flow of lukewarm air from the slowly heating engine.

An enormous gust of wind shook the car and he skidded slightly on the icy road. *Better hold the thing in second gear. Funny driving through hell in second gear, spatter of hail on the windshield but everlasting fire behind you. Wait now, for the horned gentleman with goat's legs and a trident. Watch it, Denning, watch it! You're becoming hysterical, a little more like that and you'll start gibbering—but, oh God, what the hell has happened?*

At that moment a curt voice which seemed to come from the empty seat beside him said: "Halt! Halt! Police!"

Fortunately Denning was already slowing or he would have run straight into the back of the thing which appeared suddenly in front of him.

He braked violently and stopped.

The thing was black, pear-shaped and without visible door or windows. It hung, silently, just in front of him without visible means of support.

9

As he watched, an opening appeared in the thing's side and a man stepped out. He wore what appeared to be a black crash-helmet with a sharply pointed peak. Above the peak, painted in thick, rather clumsy, white lettering were the words ZONAL POLICE. Below the helmet was a tight fitting scarlet uniform which covered the man's entire body, including his hands and feet.

He strode over and Denning automatically wound down the window, shivering in a sudden blast of ice cold air.

"Permit!" The policeman extended a scarlet-clad hand. He had a long, thinly bitter face and tiny, unpleasantly brittle blue eyes.

"My driving license, you mean?" Even to himself, Denning sounded hoarse, terrified and almost inaudible.

"Driving license?" The policeman smiled bitterly with one side of his mouth. "Friend, I am not here to play jolly guessing games, or indulge in idle banter. You are inter-zone, between frontiers, and you are not allowed out of your zone without a permit. You know the law as well as I, so now that I have wasted valuable time spelling it out for you to avoid a misunderstanding, you will produce the permit—yes?"

Denning made frantic and helpless gestures with his hands. "I don't know where I am. I think I lost my way somehow. I don't know what you mean by a permit or a zone—" His voice trailed away.

The policeman looked at him and smiled. It was a mockingly soothing smile, and it made Denning go cold inside.

"We are jesting, yes?" The smile was tigerish now. "We are daring and filled with bravado." The policeman put his hand inside the window and pointed his finger, the tip of which terminated in a bright metal point. "I, too, play games. I, too, can be the great comedian." He looked at the other thoughtfully. "I should burn a small black hole in your right ear, perhaps? It is an amusing game among jesters, but you would have to keep very still or the small black hole might be burned right through your head. Shall we begin now or would you like to produce the permit?"

"Look, I'm very sorry." Denning was almost in tears. "Please understand—" He stopped. The policeman had thrust his head into the car and was studying the instruments disbelievingly. "Mother of Sin," he said in a shocked undertone.

He withdrew his head and walked slowly around the car, studying it. Twice he kicked the tires, three times he looked underneath, then he returned. "What, in the name of God, is this thing?"

"It's"— Denning cleared his throat nervously—"It's a Ford Classic."

"Where did you get it—dig it out of a glacier?"

"I bought it four months ago."

"It's a mockup, surely. Let's look at the energy unit."

"Ener—?" Denning understood suddenly and dutifully released the hood catch.

The policeman raised it and studied the engine. "Naked Sin, it really *is* a combustion unit." He strode suddenly to the window. There was something gleaming in his hand that was clearly a weapon, and his face was ugly. "What sort of stunt is this? No more jokes, my friend. You have exactly ten seconds to tell the whole story."

"The whole story has yet to be told," said a quiet male voice, and Denning saw the policeman stiffen.

"Don't do anything rash, my friend. There are six burners pointed at the middle of your back."

"So it was a joke after all." The policeman looked at Denning with something akin to respect, then his face contorted. "What shall I do?"

"If you are wise," said the voice, "You will climb back into your prowl and go away. Forget this. It is none of your business."

"I cannot do that. You know I cannot do it. At the first

opportunity I must call for assistance, outwit you, or fight it out."

"Then you are a fool."

"True, but I cannot help it. It is the conditioning, you understand. I cannot help it."

"Then we are very sorry." There was a brief flash of violet light. The policeman stiffened. For a few seconds he stood swaying, bubbling sounds came from his throat, then abruptly he crumpled sideways.

Denning saw him clutch at the car, fall half over, his head striking the hood, and then he disappeared from view.

A voice said, "Pick him up and toss him in his prowl. He'll freeze to death out here."

"We could do with a few less of these creeps."

"We have no fight with the Z.P. and, in any case, they cannot help it."

"This one can talk."

"So can his dead body to science. Do as I say and put him in his prowl. Imagine the hornet's nest we'll stir up with a dead Z.P."

"Oh, very well, but one day——" The unseen speaker moved away and Denning lost the rest of the sentence.

The car was suddenly surrounded by dark-clad, be-goggled figures strangely resembling frogmen, and the door was wrenched open.

A begoggled head appeared, a shoulder and a hand. The hand held something glinting and metallic which looked like a weapon.

"All right, Denning, get out. We haven't much time."

"Look here, what——?"

The weapon jerked menacingly. "Out, I said. Out, out, *out*."

He climbed out, already shivering with cold again. Behind the car was a black sphere like a rigid gas balloon with a lighted opening like a door in the side.

Something prodded into his back. "In there, and *move*. We're in a hurry."

He was almost pushed through the opening, but before he could get a look at the interior a voice said, "Sorry about this, Denning, but it has to be done."

It seemed that something touched him lightly on the back of the neck. A touch which left a curious spreading numbness, sapping his strength. He swayed, clutching wildly for some sort of support, and a vague impression that someone caught him before he fell. . . .

"Are you all right, sir?" Something was shaking his shoulder gently, and he opened his eyes.

"All right? Er—yes. Yes, thank you." He was looking at a real policeman in the familiar blue uniform.

It had been a dream, *all* of it a dream. There was the shelter, the winding road and the metal sign which said, correctly: *Bus Stop.* Parked some thirty feet down the road was a police car with the comforting blue lamp on the roof. A real policeman, the familiar road, the sun shining from a cloudless sky. Yes, yes, a dream—thank God.

"You were slumped over the wheel, sir." The red face beneath the blue peaked cap was concerned. "I wondered if you had been taken ill."

"Er—no. No." Denning could have embraced him with relief. "As a matter of fact, I had been driving for some hours, felt drowsy and decided to pull off the road for a rest."

The policeman nodded. "Wish a few more drivers would use the same common sense, sir, save a lot of accidents. Glad you're all right, sir." He saluted and went away.

Denning waited until the police car was out of sight, then opened the door, climbed out and stretched luxuriously.

13

A dream, a particularly vivid dream, but, thank——
his arms, still half-raised from the stretch, went suddenly
rigid.

The car had a dent in the hood, and there were several
long scratches on the offside front fender. From beneath
the fender, water dripped steadily from a small but visible
accumulation of rapidly melting sludge. . . .

Chapter Two

Denning climbed back into the car, shakily, and tried to think. It was not so easy as he imagined. His mind appeared to have developed a peculiar disinclination to refer to the events of the past few hours. It was an almost automatic reaction, similar to a bereaved person's refusal to recall the face of the loved one because the memory brought immediate pain.

Desperately he chain-smoked his way through a packet of cigarettes. Why had he come down here, heading towards this small country town he had known as a child? Escape? Escape from what? There was no point in it; his foster parents had both been dead for years and to return now would do nothing but awake a seething nostalgia and a host of sentimental recollections. His foster parents, he recalled, had treated him lovingly as their own, but he had been found abandoned on a public house doorstep in the early hours of the morning.

Funny how vividly he could recall so much of his childhood. Strange, too, how clearly he now seemed able to think on any subject but—his mind shied away from it. He would get it sorted out later, perhaps. No doubt there was an explanation of some kind, a pity he couldn't think of a satisfactory one.

His mind turned again to the reasons for his journey. It was not only the conditions at home; there had been something curiously compulsive about everything, an urge, something almost migratory—was there such a word?—which he couldn't explain.

It wasn't Marian. He was a little shaken to find that he

could now look back on her infidelities without anger or particular regret. He was like a man touching a once-aching tooth with his tongue, startled to find no soreness or stab of pain.

He was surprised also that he felt very little about Beacham. Almost he pitied him. Beacham was not the man he appeared; true, he was physically strong, but his sexual appetites were grossly exaggerated.

He was a man with an inferiority complex somewhere deep in his character which he had to hide. Beacham drank whiskey, smoked a pipe, followed sport and womanized because he thought it was manly. He had to prove his virility both to himself and to the world. He had to have conquests not so much from animal desire but because sexual conquest eased his basic sense of insecurity.

Denning blinked, wondering how he knew and wondering even more how he knew he was right. Since the events of the last few hours he seemed to have developed a curious clarity of mind and a deep insight which he could not remember having experienced before.

Again, he seemed to have a deeper understanding of himself.

He sighed, forcing himself not to think. Better get some gas on the way back. He hoped he didn't start seeing things again, but he'd have to take that chance.

Half an hour later he pulled in at a wayside gas station to replenish the nearly empty tank.

The girl attendant, a heavily made-up blonde of about twenty-five, seemed to spend an inordinate amount of time on the car. She cleaned the screen, the windows and the headlights.

"Oil, sir?"

"I don't think so, thanks. Filled up yesterday."

"Going far, sir?"

"Quite a distance."

"We serve light meals, sir. I mean, I thought if you

16

were going a good way it might be a good idea to have something solid. We serve quite good hot meals, and you won't even have to get out, sir. We bring everything out on a tray." She looked at him. It was not the kind of look he had expected from an attendant, and he was shocked to find a response in himself. Her figure was good and nicely rounded, and the flesh on her arms—he brought himself up short. What the devil was the matter with him now? He had never been overtempted by sex and always resisted minor temptation without particular effort, but now——

"I finish at five," she volunteered. "I live in that little bungalow you can just see through the trees there. If you'd like a proper meal, home cooked, I mean——" She let the rest of the sentence hang, but there was no mistaking the implication of her words. "I'm all alone," she said.

He was tempted to say, "Do you make a habit of this sort of thing?" but checked himself in time. She didn't. He knew she didn't, and again he was fighting a losing battle with himself. A battle so violent that he began to have a sneaking sympathy for those he had hitherto regarded as incorrigible roughs. He hadn't known it was like this, an appalling hunger which forced rightness from one's mind and made morals an unattainable ideal.

Desperately he thrust some notes into the girl's hand and drove away.

He was afraid to look back, even in the driving mirror.

There were other incidents on the way home. A striking dark-haired girl in a sports car, clearly of good family and upbringing, who kept passing and repassing. Superficially she was challenging him to a race, but her smile as she drew level and the brazen invitation in her eyes suggested a different challenge altogether.

He arrived at his home shaken, conscious of new violent urges and a strange restlessness.

When he entered, Beacham was sprawled in an easy

17

chair with Marian perched on the arm running her fingers through his hair.

Neither of them moved, but Beacham, a glass of whiskey in his hand, made a mock toast and said, "Evening, sonny boy."

Denning stood still, waiting for his stomach to tighten painfully as it had done the previous week in much the same situation. Waited for ice to press against his temples, for his breath to shorten, for the thudding of his own heart and the rending emotions of shame, rage and terror.

There was nothing. He was calm, dispassionate and very nearly indifferent.

He said to Beacham, "My home, my chair, my whiskey and my wife. That's not only greedy, but damnably bad manners."

"Eh?" Beacham looked nonplussed, then he smiled unpleasantly. "Going to do something about it?"

Denning looked at him and was suddenly strangely aware of the other's feelings. Beacham was angling for a showdown because he had a conscience. His affair with Marian had been an invitation, not a conquest, and his subsequent exposure by the supposedly outraged husband a dismal anticlimax. Denning's weakness, his obvious terror, had shamed Beacham and denied him the right to prove his manhood. It had been like taking milk from a baby, and now he wanted desperately to justify himself.

"Well?" he said.

A strange calmness seemed to envelop Denning. "Out, or I throw you out—plain enough for you?"

"You and who else?" Beacham drained his whiskey.

Later, Denning was unable to say why he behaved as he did or why, doing it, he felt no doubt or qualms.

He walked—he did not stride—to the chair, leaned forward and grasped the front of Beacham's shirt. Then he jerked the arm backwards, and Beacham came out of the chair like a bundle of feathers. He came so easily that

18

Denning almost lost his balance, and then the other's face was a few inches from his own.

For a few seconds Beacham's eyes stared into his in uncomprehending disbelief, and then the disbelief slowly gave way to fury and he swung his fist.

Denning let go of the shirt, never quite understanding what prompted his action, and hit the other not with his clenched fist but his open hand.

Strangely Beacham disappeared, and Denning had a confused impression of his body sliding across a small occasional table on his left and landing heavily on the opposite side.

For a brief moment everything seemed to freeze and he had a curious cameralike impression of seeing the room in tableau. Marian, rigid, hair in disorder, staring with protruding eyes, one hand pressed tightly to her mouth, the other gripping the back of the chair as if to support herself.

An overturned vase lying precariously at the very edge of the table, flowers strewn on the carpet, the faint but steady impact of water dripping from the table to the floor.

There was a groan, a hand appeared and moved backwards and forwards across the table like some blind thing seeking purchase, and then Beacham struggled to his knees and stared at them blindly. "You bastard!" His nose looked flattened and shapeless, blood from both nostrils ran over his lips, down his chin and dripped onto his shirt.

Slowly he staggered to his feet, nearly lost his balance and clutched at the bright window curtain to support himself. It gave way and fell across his arm and shoulder so that he looked for a moment like a grotesque gladiator in a bright flowered toga.

He shrugged it off and leaned against the wall, panting. When he opened his mouth, Denning could see only the bloody gum which had held his upper front teeth.

"I'll kill you for this, Denning. By God, I'll kill you."
He staggered forward, his right arm suddenly raised and
clutched in his hand was a half-empty whiskey bottle.

Denning clutched at the arm to defend himself and,
strangely, Beacham screamed. "Let go, for God's sake, let
go!" His face was twisted in agony, and the bottle fell to
the floor.

Surprised, Denning let go.

Beacham fell to his knees, held the injured arm to his
stomach with his left hand and rocked slowly backwards
and forwards, moaning.

"You've broken my arm, you bastard, crushed it. I felt
it splinter."

Denning could see beads of sweat on the other's forehead and temple.

"Ring for a doctor or something, damn you."

"Right." Denning reached for the telephone. He felt
sorry for Beacham in a way, but it wasn't his fault, was it?
He'd only gripped to defend himself and, as for the man's
face, clearly he must have struck the table as he fell.

"You can ring for the police, too, while you're about it.
I'll have you for assault if it's the last thing I do."

Denning paused in the act of dialing. "As you wish. If
you prefer this matter in the open, we'll have it that way.
I'll leave it to you to explain the circumstances."

Beacham moaned and spat obscene words; then he became almost pathetic. "All right, drop it. You're one of
these clever ones, bide your time, get a chap over a barrel,
then kick him when he's down."

Denning felt a sudden surge of anger. It was grossly un-
just. It was——there was a crumpling sound, and he froze.

Slowly he opened his hand. Pieces of plastic fell to the
floor, and he saw that the mouthpiece of the telephone was
held only by a section of colored wire.

He stared at the ruined instrument without comprehension. He'd only gripped a little tighter in brief irritation,

20

surely not enough to——? He had only gripped Beacham's arm, and the man had gone backwards over the table. How then could he have made such a mess of his face? Again, he had only struck with an open hand, barely hard enough to draw blood from an abnormally sensitive nose.

He said in a high, unreal voice, "The phone is broken, I'd better go to the call box."

Outside, he tried to think. He exercised regularly at mild noncompetitive sports and had always been fairly fit but never robust. He tried to fight against the obvious conclusion and failed. Something had happened. The dream, the illusion or whatever it was had brought about certain changes, some obvious, some subtle. He had never been attractive to women and, generally speaking, undersexed, but now—he had a brief hungry picture of the blonde at the filling station and pushed her memory hastily from his mind. No, not that as well; he had already nearly killed a man with a blow from an open hand. What would he do next?

They—the people in the dream—had done something to him. *Sorry about this, Denning, but it has to be done.*

What had to be done—not merely rendering him unconscious, surely? No, there was no doubt whatever, that he had undergone physical and psychological changes in that period.

Why?

The unavoidable conclusion was that they had reasons for changing him. It followed also that the changes were for their benefit and not his. No group of people, however eccentric, would go to such lengths unless they expected to get something out of it.

It began to look like some sort of cat's-paw scheme. He was an adapted instrument, reshaped for specific ends and, in that case, they'd probably use him whether he liked it or not.

Shaking a little, he began to dial for the doctor. All he

21

could do at the moment was wait; no doubt they'd come for him when he was wanted.

He returned to the house almost in a daze, scarcely aware of what went on around him.

The doctor arrived, and he heard Beacham relate a palpably false account of his "accident." "Caught my foot in the carpet, head first into the fireplace, hit the bars face first, must have caught my arm at the same time."

It was clear that the doctor didn't believe him. The various injuries were inconsistent with such a fall, but it was not his business to say so. Finally, he sent for an ambulance and Beacham was taken away nursing his arm.

That was when the storm broke. As soon as the door closed, Marian began. He was a monster, a brute and a sadist. It was true, of course, he had some justification, but so had she. If he hadn't been so cold, so unfeeling, indifferent, etc., etc. After all she was only human, a woman needed affection, she needed love.

After five minutes working on that angle, she was making it sound as if he had driven her into an act of adultery at the point of a gun.

He sat down finally with his back to her and let the words flow past him unheard.

After a long time she stopped.

Denning rose and ground out his cigarette. "Is that all?" He had the certain feeling that a great deal of it had been a verbal smoke screen behind which she had retired for some entirely different end.

"What else can I say?"

He shrugged, seeing that she was about to work herself into tears. "Quite. You seem to have covered everything in triplicate."

"You beast."

He ignored the remark. "I'll get something to eat at the cafe down the road. They're open until eleven."

At the door she ran after him, clutching his arm, and then he knew what her end was.

"Must it end like this?" She looked up at him. "Darling, I'm truly sorry. We could begin again, make a fresh start." She pressed her body against his, but for her he felt only revulsion.

"I'm sorry. Had you been honest I could have forgiven you, but you are not even honest with yourself."

"I don't know what you mean."

"Then I'll tell you. You justify everything; you do not say this is my nature and I will control it or, alternatively, I'll give rein and enjoy it. Instead, you blame others for your excesses. I can forgive the wanton, but not the hypocrite."

When he came back an hour later, she was waiting by the door. Her face was flushed, her hair disheveled and her lips so thin they looked almost bloodless.

"You preaching creep, you hypocrite——" She stopped, trying to find words.

He sighed. "Now what?"

She leaned forward. "I suppose you've never heard of Linda Munson. Go on, say it, say you've never heard of her."

"All right, if it makes you any happier."

"Oh, I knew you'd deny it." She laughed shrilly. "What are you going to do when you see her—pretend she's a stranger? I doubt very much if she'll back you up, Richard. She was very determined to come in and wait."

She paused and smiled unpleasantly. "Perhaps you told her you were single, or is she pregnant by you?"

He looked at her. "Where is she?"

"In the front room. It's a nice thing having your mistress force herself into——"

"Shut up," he said.

"Look, if you think you can talk to me like——" She looked into his eyes and was suddenly stricken silent. Her

23

face paled, and she backed away. "Don't look at me like that, for God's sake. You frighten me."

He brushed past her, barely conscious that she was there, and went into the next room.

"Who the hell are you?" he said.

The woman, curled up like a cat in the wide easy chair, looked up at him and smiled. She had wide dark eyes, a clear, almost ivory, complexion and wavy chestnut-colored hair which fell almost to her shoulders. He guessed her age as twenty-eight to thirty. The petite, but full-breasted body looked as if it had been poured into the tightly fitting black dress.

"I'm Linda Munson," she said.

"Perhaps you would be good enough to explain."

"But of course. I was sent to look after you. You see I am from Firma. Firma is my world—Terra Firma, you follow me? You call this world Earth and, sometimes, Terra Firma. We call our planet Firma and, on very rare occasions, Earth. It is one of the variations between almost identical planets."

"I haven't the faintest idea what you're talking about. I have never heard of Firma."

She smiled, but there was something in her eyes that was very close to compassion. "I'm afraid this may come as a shock to you, but there is no other way to say it—you were on Firma only a few hours ago."

Chapter Three

Denning swallowed and lowered himself carefully into the nearest chair, conscious of coldness chilling his entire body.

"It was real—it actually occurred?"

"It actually occurred." Her voice was very gentle.

"This change in me—they did that?"

"It was not quite a change. They removed the mental blocks which prevented your being your true self. The blocks were there for your protection until you reached maturity."

He said bitterly, "Thanks very much. So my conclusions early this evening were correct. They, whoever 'they' are, shaped an instrument and now they want to use it. Very nice, very practical, save for the minor consideration that the instrument doesn't care for the experiment."

She said softly. "We understand that. We knew it would be hard, Richard, but please don't jump to conclusions until you've heard the full explanation."

"Very well. I'm open to an explanation, but I don't have to go along with it."

She said, "Here?"

He realized that Marian had entered the room and was looking at him with a mixture of fear and resentment.

He rose. "I have to go out." He gave no reasons and no apology.

Marian shrank back as he brushed past, her eyes filled with hatred, but she made no sound.

Twenty minutes later, Denning was alone with Linda. She had booked a pleasant and rather expensive suite at a nearby hotel.

He sat down heavily and said: "Well?"

She smiled and shook her head. "It's very difficult to know where to begin, but perhaps some background detail would be good." She paused and curled herself up in the opposite chair. "I have to simplify this, which is difficult because I don't really understand the theory myself. It is like trying to explain relativity without mathematics; this is not Einstein, however, but Brethanger, a scientist born on Firma about two hundred years ago. The Brethanger postulates, as they were called, were scorned when he first made them public, but within ten years they were beginning to be accepted as a major breakthrough in respect of what we choose to call eternity. In short, Brethanger defined infinity. His theory of time-space perceives eternity as a series of interwoven repetitive cycles." She paused and smiled. "I see you understand about as well as I am able to tell it, so I will explain as it was explained to me. You have seen those toys in which one toy is contained within another?"

"Oh yes, I know what you mean. It's usually a wooden doll which unscrews and contains another wooden doll and so on."

"Exactly, only in this case one moves from the center to the circumference. One starts with the tiny doll in the center and moves outward to a larger doll which varies only slightly from the first. In this example, however, the words 'center' and 'circumference' are relative only to time-space."

Denning lit a cigarette. "I get the outline, but I am still in a fog. Just where do I fit into—what was the word—a postulate?"

"Give me time, please. I'm not quite finished. Come back to the innermost doll and see this innermost doll as your own universe. That universe does not end but repeats itself, as in the next doll and so on."

He exhaled smoke hissingly. "I begin to get the drift. This is what you mean by a repetitive cycle."

"Exactly. The universe repeats itself, varying slightly with each repetition, to infinity which, confusing as it may sound, is also the end and the beginning. You could illustrate, for simplification, with a pearl necklace. Count from the first pearl and when you get to the last you have arrived again at the first."

Denning said, "All right, as a theory I'll ride with it. What next?"

She laughed softly. "Now we come to the core. You have a sun containing Earth and other planets in its system, beyond the solar system, the universe. If you traveled to the limits of the universe, you would pass into the beginning of its repetition. You might say to yourself, 'I am back where I started,' but in actual fact you would only have passed to the next repetitive cycle. In that cycle, you would find a third planet in a solar system which almost exactly corresponds to Earth—*we call that planet Firma.*"

Denning nearly dropped his cigarette and burned his thumb retrieving it. "Earth has a double?"

"More or less; it varies only in degree. Life started in almost precisely the same way, and language began from a similar basis. The only real difference is in age—twins, of course, never being born at precisely the same time. We are, therefore, about fifteen hundred years ahead of you, or, if you prefer it, fifteen hundred years of our recorded history has yet to be written for Earth."

"Your history is exactly the same?" He was surprised to find himself accepting this apparent fantasy as truth.

She shook her head. "There are variations. So it would be unwise in the extreme to predict your future by studying our past. We are identical twins, yes, but the fingerprints and retina patterns of identical twins vary. For example, in our history, in 1944, a man called Adelf Heuller—note the name variation—succeeded in conquering the entire

27

Western world, including the Americas. His strength, however, was spread too thinly, and within ten years his conquering armies were wholly absorbed by the subject races. Within fifteen, his nation was a minor principality, the rest administered by a dozen nations.

"Again, Firma exploded her first nuclear device in the pan-Asiatic war in 1947. It was, however, a hydrogen weapon, thus different from your first atomic weapon detonated at a slightly earlier date." She paused with a slight frown of concentration. "On Earth there is Mexico, on Firma Chexico. On Firma there are or, more aptly were, the Panama Straits; you, however, had to dig a canal. No doubt the next planetary duplicate in the repetitive cycle varies even more, but that we cannot tell. We can manipulate time-space to move from the circumference to the center, but not from the center to the circumference."

He stiffened. "You didn't come by spaceship. I imagined——" His voice trailed away and he did not complete the sentence.

She shook her head quickly. "We used the Brethanger applications which define the immediacy of identical planets as relatively infinitesimal." She paused and smiled. "It's a sort of matter-transmitter which warps the continuum between our two worlds."

"You have had space travel, I take it?"

"Oh yes." She nodded thoughtfully. "We had space travel," she frowned, her eyes suddenly dreaming. "We had space travel, we wore our solar system as a brooch and fashioned a diadem of stars." She stopped, then said with sudden bitterness, "All that was a long time ago. Today we are a divided people; today we must study science in secret and steal from star to star as secretly as ghosts."

Denning lit another cigarette, his eyes narrow and bitter. "I'm beginning to understand. Somewhere there is violence and revolution, and somehow, in some way, I am a pawn in the game. Your political affairs are not my concern and, from what I can understand, not even in my dimension. Nonetheless, because I fulfill, with some manipulation, certain requirements needed by one side or the other I am to be thrown into the conflict regardless." He exhaled smoke. "Even here, on this—to you—primitive planet, we are, at least, given a verbal gesture, the chance to be called *volunteers.*"

"Please, Richard." Her eyes were suddenly misted with tears. "It isn't like that. You are almost right, but not quite. Yes, there is revolution. We do need you, and, yes, you are special, very special, but we couldn't *ask* for your cooperation." She paused, her face troubled, apparently searching for words. "Oh God, please understand. I'm only an agent; my orders permit me to tell you only so much. The rest you must learn, experience, and reason about when the time comes."

He rose, crossed to the window and stood staring down at the street. Somehow it had become garish, unreal and peopled with puppets. Puppets who walked the streets, drove cars, held hands and gestured with their mouths. Puppets who had no idea that up here was a man involved in the political strife of a world beyond their comprehension.

He turned slowly back to the room. "So I'm special, so special they send one woman—why?"

She made a tiny, almost imperceptible gesture with her shoulder. "I was least likely to be missed; there are frequent spot-checks on the men. Again, we knew what would happen."

"Knew what would happen. What the hell does that mean?"

She met his eyes directly. "We knew that you would need a woman. Is that plain enough?"

He felt himself coloring. She had said the words directly, without the faintest trace of embarrassment, but there was no mistaking her meaning.

He swallowed. "Good God, you know I've—" He stopped, unable to find words. Then he said, "To hell with you," and strode for the door.

She anticipated his move and was there before him. "I'm sorry, Richard." Something gleamed in her hand. "I don't want to freeze you, but I will if I have to."

He looked at her and at the weapon in her hand and sighed. He couldn't win, could he? Even if he got clear now, sooner or later they'd catch up with him again.

He shrugged. "All right, you win. What now?"

She smiled. "That's better." She put away the gun. "Please sit down."

He sat. "How do you know I won't jump you?"

She laughed softly. "You'd never make it, not even you. Watch." Her hands were well away from her body but quite suddenly the weapon was back in her palm and pointing straight at his heart. "You see?"

He nodded sourly. "I see." He lit another cigarette. "What is this? Seduction at gun point?"

She laughed with genuine amusement. "Are you suggesting I need a gun to awaken *you?*"

He tensed. "God, you bitch!"

"Don't try it." The gun was back in her hand again.

He forced himself to relax. "Sorry."

"Please, I am not taunting you."

"It sounded very much like it to me."

"It was not intended that way. We knew what the changes would be when the blocks were removed. Understandably, with your Terran social background, you are shocked by your unfamiliar urges." She sighed. "Truly, Richard, I wish I could tell you why, but I can't, not yet. It would have been easier for you on Firma where the link between the physical and psychological are part of the normal education and where, to quote from a social axiom, 'A man is as moral as his glandular make-up permits.' "

30

She paused and sighed again. "The civilization in which you have grown up is still, unfortunately, weighed down with taboos, inhibitions and rigid misconceptions. To quote again, 'Virtue is only virtue when it contributes, not when it inhibits.' "

He managed to grin twistedly. "Very well, I stand to be appeased. You have other reasons for being here, I take it?" She nodded. "Yes. You may be in danger. I am not exactly a bodyguard, but I am armed and familiar with the type of weapons which may be used."

"I take it, in the event of such danger, I am the primary target? Don't bother to answer that question, I can see the answer in your eyes. As a matter of curiosity, why? If I am going to be killed I'd like to know the reasons and who will be responsible."

She shook her head quickly. "It will have to be brief. It is the age-old struggle for freedom. You represent a factor which may spell liberation."

"Sweet words which are easily distorted and, too often, have opposite meanings—who is the oppressor?"

She frowned slightly at the contempt in his voice but answered him directly. "We are a people divided by physical circumstance and tactical advantage. There are two oppressors, the aliens and their collaborators. Our direct concern, yours and mine, is with the collaborators."

"There is, of course, an arch collaborator?"

Again she chose to ignore his contempt. "Yes, I'm afraid there is. Paulus Kostain, Minister of Internal Security."

"He has, needless to say, been advised of my existence."

She chose to take his words seriously. "Not advised, but we fear he has enough to go on to draw the right conclusions——"

Minister Kostain had not drawn quite the right conclusions, but he had a clear enough lead to order a general

31

roundup of certain suspects in the 'underground.' Most of the captives were 'psyched' as an anti-interrogation precaution, but Kostain had the resources of a master race at his disposal and the psychiatric teams got down to their work with the efficiency of long practice. Breaking down hypnotically-imposed mental resistance is not a pleasant procedure and five of the suspects died before the experts learned the correct application. The survivors, before they went insane, gave enough information to provide an outline if not a complete picture of events.

"Clever." Kostain might have been mildly applauding a successful move in chess. "In fact, quite neat, for a Lolly-inspired project. You get the point, don't you, Tovin? These creatures knew perfectly well that with all our detectors they had no hope of building any effective weapon, so they went into something new—biogenetics."

"Quite, sir." After years of practice, Tovin had brought the inflections of profound respect to a supreme art. He could switch those inflections now from astonished admiration to sincere agreement without having to think about it. His last two words could be defined as a perfect balance between comprehension and gratitude that his superior saw fit to confide in him. It was also a safely neutral comment which in no way committed him to clarify his opinions.

Kostain was not deceived and never had been. While Tovin remained the highly efficient official he was, Kostain could tolerate his ingratiating foibles without irritation.

"I'll explain what we've concluded." Kostain drew a paper towards him and began to make swift notes as he spoke. "The Lolly specialists have created by genetic means a man-thing or, more likely, a man-extraordinary. As far as we can gather, two were created and there is no doubt whatever the job was really special. Their creations took two generations of genetic manipulation to bring to perfection. We know what they did with one. They switched him to Earth as a child and allowed him to grow to maturity there. The policeman's report, the power discharges recorded on our instruments, the incident in the neutral zone, all confirm that. It appears, therefore, that last week they brought him here, made some necessary adjustments and used the Brethanger applications, to switch him back to what they hope is a safe hide-out. We shall, needless to say, have to send someone to take care of him."

"And the other one, sir?" Tovin was alert and intense now like a hound which has caught the first scent of the quarry.

"That, alas, we do not know. The information is so widely dispersed among the hundreds involved in the project that it will probably take a year of continuous interrogation to arrive at the truth. They have been smart, you see. Each knows a little and no more." He looked up. "Tovin, we cannot afford to wait a year."

Tovin nodded soberly. "If we could catch Viegler, sir."

"If there is a Viegler. It may be a false lead put out by Lolly propaganda."

"Could be, sir, but I could find out for certain—given a free hand."

"You'd love that, wouldn't you?"

Tovin in some respects was an honest man. "Yes, sir, I would."

"Very well. I'll explain the situation and try and get official sanction."

"Thank you, sir." Tovin frowned. "These two 'things,' sir. What are they—supermen?"

Kostain stroked his chin thoughtfully. "Frankly, Tovin, that question worries me because I don't know the answer." He drummed his fingers on his desk. "We must, however, be circumspect and use our intelligence. In the first place, what do we mean by superman? If we presuppose a super intelligence we may be overreaching ourselves. Even a super intelligence needs power units for the

33

construction of super weapons. The application of those power units, however, could be instantly detected and thus defeat the ends for which the superman was created."

"A tactical superman, sir?" Tovin had rare flashes of inspiration. "A man created for the coordination of all forces in the event of an uprising?"

Kostain nodded. "I'd ride with that but for one thing. To fight successfully, an army needs something more than side arms. In this case, it also needs numerical superiority." He sighed. "We must consult experts on this matter before committing ourselves to further speculation."

He paused, frowning, then changed the subject abruptly. "What is my next appointment?"

"Mark Liston, sir." Tovin had a prodigious memory. "The subject for deportation."

"Ah, yes, Liston. Hand me his file, please."

Chapter Four

Kostain went through the file quickly to satisfy himself once again that Liston had no relatives in high positions or influential friends. This weeding and elimination process had to be done with a great deal of discretion. The Cotemps, the privileged class he outwardly represented, must, as long as possible, regard him as their protector, not an executioner.

Kostain closed the file and smiled to himself. An excellent choice. Tovin had done a good and thorough job as usual.

Liston's parents were both dead, and Liston had estranged most of his friends by becoming a little too intimate with their wives, mistresses or daughters. It was abundantly clear also that Liston was something of a character, a harmless one, but a character. He painted, wrote verse and had the temerity to think for himself. Yes, it was an excellent choice. The zone would benefit by his departure.

Kostain leaned back in his chair and smiled. He had a pale, almost beautiful, face and a curious quirk at the left hand corner of the perfectly chiseled mouth. The eyes were pale, in some lights almost colorless, and the thick red hair was a mass of tiny curls pressed so close to his scalp that the general effect looked like a crew cut.

Kostain was youthful, six feet in height, slender and exquisitely tailored. He looked cultured, aloof but never menacing.

The danger lay in his complete single-mindedness. He was tireless, frighteningly intelligent and completely detached. Kostain recognized no loyalty to state, deity or individual, loved power for its own sake and believed only in himself.

He had seen, as soon as he was old enough to reason, that the road to power lay only through whole-hearted collaboration and now, at the age of thirty-two, he held a position of power which would have put the ancient dictators to shame.

He made a slight movement with his fingers which was instantly picked up and "recognized" by hidden receptors.

A respectful voice said, "Yes, sir?"

"Send in ex-director Liston."

"At once, sir."

A few seconds later, Liston entered. He was a tall, fair-haired man with obvious charm and sleepy-looking blue eyes, whose laughter lines in the corners made him look deceptively indolent.

Kostain waved him to a chair, made sure that he was seated and read the official charges. They were all trivial but so carefully slanted and so pompously phrased that they sounded like capital offenses. Similar omissions occurred every day, but the authorities turned a blind eye unless, as now, it was expedient to do otherwise.

Kostain asked him if he understood the charges.

Liston smiled faintly. "No. Do you?"

"This is not a joking matter," said Kostain coldly.

"Ah, that I appreciate. One is not honored by such high authority, however minor the offense, unless the penalty is capital—correct? In short, expedience demands my removal but you have to cook up some misdemeanors for public consumption."

Kostain looked at him with a mixture of respect and disapproval. They were getting rid of this one just in time. Liston was just a little too smart for his own safety. He said, smoothly and with a faint smile, "Some people like the

36

formalities, Liston. It ensures their self-respect. It appears, however, that you prefer the naked truth."

"I don't prefer it, but I cannot believe I was brought here for fun. What is the sentence?"

Kostain shrugged and made no attempt to soften the blow. "Deportation."

"Oh, so!" Liston whistled softly. "Have I any choice— in which direction I am deported, I mean?"

"Traditionally the choice is yours."

"How nice! You could oblige me with the loan of a coin, perhaps?"

Kostain's pale eyes narrowed slightly, and for the first time in many years he was ruffled inwardly. "Don't crowd your luck, ex-director. A mite more insolence and I shall be compelled to select some of the alternatives to deportation." He calmed himself and looked at the other thoughtfully. "You appear to forget, Liston, that there are other charges not mentioned on the official list. A very large number of influential people, for example, have lodged complaints in respect to your—ah—affairs. In our files alone are the names of at least twenty young women who have become pregnant by you."

Liston took it easily. "That is hardly my fault, Minister. Family limitation is ridiculously easy and provided without cost."

"True. Most of these women appear completely infatuated with you, however, and refuse medical aid. It is the refusal which has caused the storm, Liston. You would have been well advised to exercise your undoubted fascination in order to change their views."

"Perhaps, but it is too late now."

Kostain sat frowning to himself long after Liston had gone. No doubt Liston had been acting. Men did act to conceal their terror, but in this case the performance had been first class. The man's hands had been steady, his whole bearing casual and almost indifferent. There were not many, faced with the notice of slow execution, who could put on a show like that.

Liston for his part was not quite so calm as he had appeared outwardly. He had, because he despised Kostain, put up a fairly good front, but it was not really clever. All his life he had possessed the peculiar ability to stand aside from himself and his emotions. Now, with no need to deceive himself or others, he was conscious of a coldness in his stomach and a curious shortness of breath.

It was difficult to adjust one's mind to one's own death. To realize that within a few hours it would be all over, one kept thinking about what one would do *after,* which, unless one had some sort of religion, was patently absurd. There was no after: one knew it but kept thinking about it. Again, one forgot, "on Tuesday I'll—" There wouldn't be another Tuesday, not for him.

He wondered if anyone would care—Trina, Marla, Jannice? They might shed a few tears. Women did that sort of thing, not necessarily because they cared but because, more or less, it was expected of them. They even expected it of themselves so, very probably, they would study their puffy eyes in the mirror later and feel they had paid him due homage.

He tried to remember the others but there were so many faces, so many bodies. God, there had been a lot, hadn't there? Twenty pregnant—so few? Security must be slipping, there must be at least——

Mark, I know it sounds crazy but I want this child, your child.

How many had said that or words very much like it—why? Why always him?

He pushed the question from his mind. It didn't matter now, it was all over. In a few hours he would be "deported" or, more aptly, removed in such a way that it would look like an accident or suicide. Not that the discerning would believe either, but it was good enough for general consumption.

This sort of thing was not new; it happened in every social upheaval. One created a privileged class and, with the passing of time, it became decadent and had to be weeded out to make room for the opportunist. In this case, however, if rumor were true, there was no opportunist, not a human one anyway.

Ah, well, in an hour or so, he would be permitted—with some prodding from the rear, no doubt—to drive to his own execution.

Two guards arrived who accompanied him to his office while he signed over his executive position to someone not stated on the official form. It was rather like signing his own death warrant and, in the middle of it, his secretary came in, began to speak, saw the two guards and was suddenly silent.

Liston found himself studying her almost impersonally. Strange, he'd never made it with her, or was it that she had never made it with him?

The naturally blond hair, scraped back from her face and laid in a heavy bun at the back of her head, gave her a forbidding appearance. She wore straight and shapeless clothes and sensible, unglamorous, wide flat shoes. Yet, somehow, despite her appearance, he had always had the inward feeling that she was all woman, warm, rounded, passionate. Good God, why? Even her name, Maria Calcott, somehow matched her appearance of dowdy sexless efficiency. She did all the work. Even the weekly chore of signing a few papers she had taken upon herself. She, of all the women he had known, was one of the few he liked as a person. Most of the others, he thought without shame, had been instruments of pleasure.

"You are ready, sir?" The expulsion guards were always studiously correct.

39

"Yes, I'm ready." He waved a casual hand at Maria. "This is good-by—thank you for everything."

She did not answer. Her eyes, which were deeply blue, looked blank and expressionless. She almost looked through him, then turned abruptly and left the room.

Liston shrugged slightly and allowed the guards to pilot him from the building.

Outside, a vehicle was waiting and one of the guards opened the door for him.

As he climbed in, he turned his head and looked up. At a medium height but close to the horizon the sun shone warmly in the sky. The sun of a late summer afternoon, in a zone where it was always late summer and the word "afternoon" was an historic rather than a familiar word. A sun which always shone from exactly the same position.

How many, he wondered, have gone before me and looked up at the sun like this?

Only a lift and flare of eyes that faced
The sun, like a friend with whom their love is done.

Once he would have remembered who wrote the lines but not now, not when——

The guards pushed him gently into the car. "Route one, sir." The door slid shut beside him. He laid his finger on the starter plate and felt the vehicle rise on its cushion of energy to its regulation nine inches above the surface of the roadway.

It looks, he thought, all very tidy and prosaic. There was nothing about the interior of the vehicle to tell him it was, to all intents and purposes, a hearse.

He sighed, switched to forward and allowed the automatics to carry him into the flow of traffic.

Two hours later, it was clear he was nearing the limits of the zone. The sun was lower in the sky, the traffic was thinner and the shadows were long and dark.

For the last twenty minutes or so, the houses had been becoming smaller, more congested and meaner. These were

40

the homes of what one might choose to call, ironically, the privileged underprivileged—the tenements of minor officials in a privileged society.

He came abruptly to the frontier, and a green light blinked him through the double force-screens without the need for him to slacken speed.

This is the beginning of the end, he thought.

Ahead of him, on either side of the highway, was a no-man's-land of rough boulder, sparse grass and crumbling ruin. Some of the ruins bore a vague resemblance to living places, but most were piles of rubble casting long black shadows in the reddish light. The sun was lower now, a red and glowing cinder resting on the roofs of the buildings which had once housed and protected him.

Ahead of him, the wide black road tapered away into the distance like black ribbon toward a horizon that was a white glittering line.

He drove on, conscious of a rising wind. Beyond the frontier were no deflectors, no invisible buffers to break the hurricanes which howled continuously across the desolation of the neutral zone.

Once, so history said, the planet Firma had revolved on its axis. There had been day and night, winter and summer, autumn and spring. That, however, had been before his time, nearly a hundred and twenty years ago. Now the rotation had stopped, had been stopped for nearly ninety years, and Firma presented only one side of her face to the sun.

On that side, the hot side, people lived by dint of sweat, science and a fingertip hold on survival. People dwelt on the cold side by the same token but both, according to his education, were lesser beings verging on the subnormal. Nonetheless, his educators had insisted, perhaps vaguely conscious that they were stretching his credulity to the limit, these people were not there as a punishment. They were there because they were incapable of adjusting to the

41

advanced culture of the privileged zone. Most of them were natural nomads and preferred their wild freedom to the ordered civilization of the temperate zone.

Understandably, only the educated, the sensitive and cultured dwelt in the temperate zone. They dwelt in it because of their cultural superiority and were, therefore, privileged by birth.

Needless to say, although the underprivileged could in no way contribute to or exist in such a society, these lesser beings were jealous of its wealth, comfort and position and plotted continuously to bring about its downfall.

Liston laughed cynically to himself. Out here it sounded phonier than it had in the classroom but, strangely, ninety percent of the society in which he had lived accepted this pretentious guff without question. Ah, well, he had been one of them, perhaps less gullible than most but, nonetheless, one of the privileged. Now he was an outcast, an ex— they used an unpleasant nickname—an ex-Co-temp, meaning a collaborator from the temperate zone.

He smiled twistedly. The Co-temps, in their turn, favored a similar childish humor. They called those on the cold side Lollies and those on the hot side Buns.

He became aware that two pear-shaped vehicles had swung in behind him and were providing a polite but pointed escort some two hundred yards to the rear. The Z.P. had arrived to make quite sure he did not try to sneak back.

The Zonal Police had always frightened Liston, perhaps because they were almost human. They protected the Co-temps, behaved normally, had families and were interested in the things that interested normal men, but their humanity stopped there. They could only act according to rules hypnotically imposed upon their brains and, in the capacity of police, were little more than organic robots.

They had been created by the Co-temps to protect the frontiers, but they were something more than that. They were an army, an army of triggermen with a vicious little energy gun concealed in the index finger of their scarlet gauntlets.

He glanced upward and saw that the sky was dark, and here and there stars were visible. The sun was now a mere arc of sullen scarlet, most of it cut by the skyline.

Ahead, the white line which had been the horizon had become a visible range of mountains, icily beautiful and reflecting the crimson of the sun.

To his right, parallel with the road, a river raced toward the sun. Here it was a welter of foam and pack-ice but, after crossing the temperate zone, it would lose itself as a trickle of steaming water in the endless sand.

He glanced at the thermometer with which the vehicle was provided. The exterior temperature was minus one degree centigrade and automatically he reached for the heater.

It wasn't there, of course; it wasn't meant to be. This was the omission which made his execution final.

He realized with sudden despair that he did not know what cold was. He knew the tingle of a cold shower, of ice cubes in a long drink, but cold, real cold, was beyond his comprehension or experience.

Hail spattered briefly against the windshield, and he sensed rather than felt the buffeting of the wind. Above, the sky was now dark but streaked with color, an aurora of pastels misting the sky and dimming the stars.

He saw that the windshield was filigreed with frost, and his breath was now visible as he exhaled.

Ahead, the mountains were now clearly revealed as glaciers, snow-capped, rising in tiers, precipice upon precipice almost to the stars.

There was a click as the standard receptor within the vehicle responded to an impulse from one of the police cars. "Attention deportee, Mark Liston. You have now crossed the frontier into the cold zone. You are not permitted to return. Any attempt to do so will be met with force—out!"

"Blast your eyes," Liston said savagely and drove on. He was slowly becoming aware that something curious was happening to his feet and hands. Both were suffering from a painful biting sensation, yet the lobes of his ears were burning unpleasantly. He realized suddenly that this was cold, a cold that sooner or later was going to kill him.

He tried to remember what he had read about the subject. One could by maintaining the circulation, that is, by violent exercise, ward off its effects for long periods. What happened when one had to stop due to exhaustion? Funny, the blood seemed to have gone from his little finger. It was numb and difficult to bend.

There was another click. "Welcome to the Cold Zone." The voice was deep, ironic and mockingly polite. "Welcome to everlasting darkness, welcome I say."

Liston blew on his numbing fingers and swore under his breath. He was now conscious of another cold—cold terror. This was not going to be a pleasant way to die.

The voice continued. "How do you like our zone? Do you find it inspiring, majestic or just plain terrifying? Whatever your reactions, try and imagine what it is like to be born, to live one's entire life, and to die here. You have sat so long warming your hands in the glow of privilege that you didn't think, didn't know and didn't care how bad it was. But you know now, don't you?"

Chapter Five

The voice paused, then continued. "Are you cold, deportee? You think you are cold, yes, but it is not truly cold. With thick clothes you could live and breathe. Out here where I am, I need an electrically heated suit. I need heated lenses to see and heated ducts through which to breathe lest my eyes turn to ice in my head and my lungs to stone in my body. Alas, you have no heated suit, have you, deportee? Too bad you did not warn us of your coming or we might, just might, have thought of bringing along a spare one."

Liston extracted a cigarette from his case with numb fingers and watched it ignite. "Gloat, you bastard," he said savagely. His teeth were now chattering uncontrollably with cold but he managed to keep his voice almost steady.

"Ah, an outcast with guts." The voice, however, was still mocking. "It is not often we get one with guts. Tell me, can you remember what warmth was like?"

Liston scowled, but he was now so cold that he dare not trust himself to speak. The interior of the windshield was now coated with ice restricting visibility to a few hundred feet.

"Answer my question, Liston. Can you remember what it was like to be warm?" The voice was no longer mocking but urgent and authoritative.

How, Liston wondered, did the other know his name?

"I asked you a question, *answer it,* man! Remember, *force yourself* to remember warmth. Your *life* depends on that memory. You must remember. You must remember and *think*. You must think that heat and cold are relative. You must think that the cold now biting into your body is an illusion; you must think that you are warm. You must think that the ice is just as warm as your sun garden in the temperate zone."

Liston, his mouth clamped tight to stop his teeth chattering, tried to make sense of the words. Was this a joke or some sort of elaborate torture to make the last minutes of his life as intolerable as possible? Think? What difference would it make? It was something to do; better to play games than to break down. *Right, my sadistic friend, I'll think. I won't give you the satisfaction of seeing or hearing me shout for help.* He was sitting in a deck chair feeling the heat of the sun, even the small icicle hanging just above the window must radiate a small amount of——

Liston arched backwards abruptly and, by supreme effort, bit back a moan. So it was a torture, a torture devised by people who knew and understood the psychology of freezing man and knew how to make it worse. He was in agony, his hands, feet, face and ears ached and throbbed intolerably. Inside he whimpered, felt himself doubling over and twisting with the pain. God, his fingers felt as if they had been struck repeatedly with a hammer. Instinctively he thrust them towards his mouth.

He was suddenly rigid. His fingers and hands were no longer white and bloodless but had almost returned to their normal color. They still hurt but the pain was slowly lessening. Abruptly he realized that he was no longer shivering, that his lower lip was sore where he had bitten it, that his teeth were no longer chattering.

With an effort he forced himself to relax and realized with incredulous disbelief that he was almost warm. He *might* be sitting in his sun garden in the temperate zone.

He glanced at the thermometer and decided he was insane or dying; the exterior temperature was minus thirty degrees centigrade.

"Nice work, Liston." The voice sounded genuinely pleased and almost friendly. "Keep straight on."

Liston felt a light-headed bubbling sense of triumph. "I'll do that, but into which glacier? There's an inch of ice on the ground of the windshield and visibility is about nine feet."

"Switch to control."

"God, do you have a control system in this wilderness?"

"We do, but only for the next few hundred miles; after that, the ice takes over everything."

"Right." Liston flicked to automatic and almost immediately felt the vehicle treble its speed. He cursed himself inwardly. Why hadn't he thought of that? At maximum, the vehicle would be in the supersonic band, and air friction would have heated the skin and perhaps beaten the cold. On the other hand, you couldn't go racing up and down a highway forever. Starving to death would be just as final as cold. Funny, he didn't feel cold anymore.

The supersonic speed continued for about two minutes and then he felt the vehicle begin to slow. Through the windshield he thought he saw lights, and the vehicle stopped.

The door opened and a rough voice said, "Out!"

"Why the hell should I?" He was suddenly belligerent. If there was a joke somewhere, it was on him.

A gloved hand appeared, and in it was a brass-colored weapon with a long flared barrel. "Out, or we burn you out—any comment?"

"None which will sound convincing." He climbed out and found himself surrounded by dark begoggled figures vaguely resembling undersea divers.

He looked about him. The mile-wide highway had narrowed to a strip only ten feet wide and terminated abruptly in a sheer cliff of ice. Ice rose on either side and above—it seemed miles up—was a tiny jagged rectangle of stars.

Something prodded into his back and a voice said, "Move."

He moved but was acutely conscious that he wore only

47

a light suit, that the temperature must be at least forty below; but to him it was cool and by no means unpleasant.

An opening appeared in the ice. He was pushed through it and, a few seconds later, he heard an airlock hiss shut behind him.

He was in a tunnel, a yellow tunnel filled with light. So that's how the Lollies lived and kept the ice at bay—Stresstacine.

Someone seemed to note his interest. "Don't imagine we've enough of this stuff to waste, Liston. We only use it in vital places—emergency exists, hospitals, experimental laboratories. About eighty-seven million of our people spend their lives praying that the ice won't shift. There's only a sprayed coating of nonconductor between them and three thousand feet of ice. Sometimes those prayers go unheard; a glacier shifts and we can only weep." The speaker paused and sighed. "Only our capital city has Stresstacine protection, a skeleton of girders, some shoring and a few emergency shelters. It will take four hundred years to build complete protection for every city."

Liston saw that the Stresstacine had now given way to gray nonconductor, a rubbery substance which served only to keep out the cold and retain the heat.

It struck him suddenly as miraculous and inconceivable that several hundred million people should live under this enormous canopy of ice. They had bored tunnels and caverns in it and lived out their entire lives in it like worms in an apple, never seeing sun or star or sky. He'd never thought about it before. When he'd thought of the Lollies he'd had vague mental pictures of igloos, of whales and fur-clad figures cutting holes in the ice. *And that,* he thought, *is exactly the kind of picture my educators wanted me to have.* If there were whales, they were frozen solid in the glaciers; as for the furs, perhaps that was the biggest joke of all. Travel another few hundred miles and the atmosphere was, no doubt, so cold that exposure to it would mean almost instant death. Only the constant convection, the winds racing from the cold side to the hot kept the atmosphere from freezing completely.

Liston was a highly intelligent man and began to curse himself for a fool. What a damned idiot he had been. He'd lapped up the stupid propaganda because he'd been too damned lazy to think for himself. Whatever the Lollies were going to do to him he deserved, not that individually he was without guilt. Soft living and far too many women had effectively kept him from using his head.

The realization of his own responsibility began to link with other unpleasant thoughts in his mind. Could it be that those persistent rumors were true? Could it be that over a century ago aliens had landed on Firma and that certain unscrupulous people had collaborated with them? It was said that alien science had stopped the planet's rotating on its axis. If so, the reason, to him at any rate, was now abundantly clear. The aliens had executed a neatly unpleasant technical trick which had successfully divided the human race into three and set them up for subsequent knockdown at the aliens' leisure.

Another thought occurred to him. The aliens and the original collaborators could have taken up residence in the temperate zone before actual stoppage occurred, couldn't they? Yes, and not only taken up residence but made thorough preparation for the inevitable physical terrors to follow. The temperate zone was, he remembered, "stressed" for earthquakes and force-barriered against flood and hurricane. A science which could stop the rotation of an entire planet could also stop that rotation exactly where it wanted.

Liston scowled to himself. Oh yes, the Co-temp zone, a mere strip a few hundred miles wide where living was tolerable and pleasant. The Co-temp zone, the privileged strip which encircled the entire planet, which physically and, for that matter, tactically, divided hot side from cold and permitted the Co-temps to play God.

He realized suddenly that the tunnel had ceased to be smooth but now contained numerous openings and intersections. He was in a Lolly city, or should it be community?

It was warm too, and his captors were already divesting themselves of goggles and helmets.

He said, to no one in particular, "Where are you taking me and why am I here?"

"In time you will meet Viegler. He will explain everything."

He was about to ask more when the thought occurred to him that above his head were several thousand feet of ice and that shifting ice was treacherous. He glanced upward uneasily and did not ask the question.

Someone seemed to read this thoughts. "It's not so bad as you might imagine, Liston—at least, not now. We've learned so much, you see. We have flaw-detectors and shift-readers, so we can predict major falls long before they occur and get the people out in time. Of course, there are occasional minor falls, but these are no more hazardous than traffic in a busy street!"

"I see." Liston was not comforted; in a busy street you could *see* traffic coming.

"Here." He was hustled suddenly through an opening in the tunnel and found himself in a long, dreary but brightly lighted gray room which contained two small plastic chairs and a large round table.

A man sat in one of the chairs behind the table. He looked up as Liston was thrust into the room.

"The prisoner, sir." There was marked respect in the voice.

"Very well, leave us. Make sure I am not disturbed."

"As you order, sir."

The man waved Liston to the remaining chair. "Please be seated."

Liston sat. The other appeared to be studying him intently, and embarrassed, he stared back.

The man at the table was not impressive. Small, myopic in appearance, he resembled a minor official in some obscure ministry. The ancient face, the untidy eyebrows, the drooping moustache—all of it added up to a nonentity, except for the eyes, small, smoldering, but brightly intelligent.

The man said, "I am Viegler. I represent, from your side of the fence, the opposition. In truth, I am the opposition."

Liston nodded because he felt something was expected of him but made no comment.

Viegler continued, his low but curiously distinct voice giving the words force. "I will not waste your time with long scientific explanations or political justification. I direct an underground movement whose aim is to save the race by overthrowing the collaborators and their alien masters. It is not a new ideal and the measures for its realization were laid down long ago, in fact in my grandfather's day."

He paused and drummed blunt nervous fingers on the table. "Liston, you are not here because we have taken pity on a collaborator, but because of what you are." Again he paused, the untidy nondescript eyebrows drawn together in a frown. "It's like this, Liston. We couldn't build weapons because they are always watching and checking, so we had to work on another line—a line less likely to arouse suspicion—biogenetics. In short, by working on a program covering three generations we have succeeded in producing a man-extraordinary, one capable, we hope, of helping to bring our dreams to fulfillment. To date, at any rate, he has succeeded in demonstrating that at least some dreams conceived by the experimenters are practical realizations."

Again he paused and looked at the other directly. "Liston, how many people do you know capable of *adapting*

51

to temperatures far below survival level?" He averted his eyes abruptly and busied himself with something on the table, as if realizing that Liston needed more than a few seconds to absorb not only his words but the implications.

After several minutes Liston said, "How the hell did I get into the Co-temp zone?"

"We put you there as a six-month-old baby." Viegler leaned back in his chair. "You must realize that we are not without an organization. A switch was effected, and the original Mark Liston was removed from a maternity hospital—you were substituted in his place."

Liston frowned. "Why?"

"Unfortunately, their counter-organization is good. They got wind of something and we had to hide you. Clearly, the safest place was in the privileged zone where they were least likely to look."

"You knew they were going to throw me out?"

"We were warned when the decision was taken. We have agents too, you know."

"They must be damned good. Today no one gets in or out without a permit."

"They don't go in or out; they stay there. All of them were introduced in the same way as yourself. We are a few steps ahead of the opposition in that respect. Our agents undergo prenatal hypno-indoctrination. The twenty-first birthday triggers off the prebirth instructions, and the agent remembers not only the truth, his contacts, but his actual mission in the zone. So far, not one has been detected."

Liston stretched in his chair. "Right, you have an organization. You also have, no doubt, a blueprint for insurrection. Where do I fit in?"

Veigler leaned forward. "Much of your task you have unwittingly completed, but there are certain mental blocks to be removed from your mind. This operation will make you something more than adaptable; you will become a man-extraordinary, possessing certain faculties not given to the normal man."

"Suppose I don't want to play?" Liston's voice was harsh.

"We think you will. We think, when you have seen and checked the evidence, you will decide for yourself."

"In respect of what?"

"Your allegiance—man or alien."

Liston said, "Perhaps," noncommittally.

Veigler shrugged faintly, then leaned forward. "Liston, too many lives and far, far too many years have gone into your creation for us to dispose of you lightly but, if we find it necessary, we shall and will write you off—is that clear?"

"Quite clear. Play, or else."

"You must understand that you are not alone." Veigler was clearly evading a showdown. "There is another one, another like you."

"A twin?"

"Not quite a twin, but another with an identical bio-genetics background."

"Really. Where did you hide him?"

Viegler ignored the implied sarcasm and answered the question directly. "Using the Brethanger applications we switched him to a corresponding Firma in the time-space repetitive cycle—a planet called Earth."

Liston, who had read extensively, felt himself pale. "Wasn't that damned dangerous?"

"It was very dangerous. The applications had never been attempted before, although, I understand, the Co-temps, with some assistance from their alien masters, have now perfected a similar device."

"What about Brethanger's parallel conclusions on compensating reflections—doesn't that propound some theory or other about the state of one finally reflecting on all the others?"

"True, we were at great pains to avoid affecting the status quo."

"Let us hope the Co-temps exercise similar care," Liston remarked. "According to Brethanger, too great an interference could set up stresses capable of destroying the entire sequence of repetitions."

"We are aware of the danger. We are also aware that ultimately the sorry state of our planet will also affect the sequence, like a rotten apple transmitting its corruption to others."

Liston nodded slowly. "You have a logical argument there."

"Our evidence pointing to alien intervention on this planet is also logical. We shall at no time appeal to your emotions. We ask only that you judge the evidence and decide for yourself."

"And if I decide in your favor?"

"You will be given the tasks for which you were created."

"And this fits in somewhere with an uprising."

"It does."

"I see." Liston rose suddenly. "Let me tell you something, Viegler, realistically and without malice. This insurrection had better be good, damned good. Do you realize that one tiny resonance bomb no bigger than a pigeon's egg could bring this whole damned ice pack down on your head?"

"I am the leader, a commander. Every commander must take calculated risks."

"Calculate them out." Liston's voice was harsh.

"I beg your pardon?" Viegler was obviously taken aback.

"If it came to the push," Liston was smiling coldly. "if it came to a showdown, *I* might have to write *you* off, and I'm not joking."

Viegler brushed the remark aside with a faint smile. "Perhaps your biogenetic twin will feel differently. By the way, his name is Denning—Richard Denning."

Chapter Six

Richard Denning was, however, less concerned with broader views and, at that moment, wholly occupied with personal problems.

He stared moodily from the hotel window and wondered where the devil it was all going to end. It was four days since Linda Munson had introduced herself at his home and inwardly he felt choked and frustrated.

Linda made him short of breath to look at her, but a problem had arisen. Denning didn't like the problem and had tried to tell himself it wasn't there—but without success. He wished to God she was the blonde at the filling station, he wished she was anyone but Linda, he wished—Hell, it wasn't that she wasn't willing. She was yielding, and inviting. The real problem was, of course, that after four days in her company it was something more than desire—he was in love with her.

Denning cursed inwardly. All right, he wanted a woman; he wanted Linda, but not that way. As far as he could make out she was doing a job as an agent for some sort of subversive organization on her own planet. He didn't want her to give herself to him in "line of duty," but because she loved him in return. If only she had said, or implied that she felt something, if only a mild affection, it might have helped; but always she was brisk, businesslike and appallingly matter-of-fact. Her friendly attitude of "if you need a woman, well, I am woman," left him angry and frustrated. It was, he felt, like procuring the services of a patriotic prostitute—not that he would have scorned the services of a professional woman at the moment—but he couldn't treat Linda like that, not now.

Denning swore horribly under his breath and turned away from the window.

Linda had gone into the bedroom while he finished his meal—he always seemed to be eating these days, perhaps it was part of whatever they had done to him.

He stared moodily at the empty plates and cutlery on the table, lit a cigarette and turned back to the window. A young girl passed by on the opposite side of the street and he jerked his eyes hastily away. God, he was developing into a monster, wasn't he? He had a brief mental picture of his own name in the paper on some unsavory sex charge and wondered with a tinge of irony what the devil he had found to think about *before* the change.

A slight sound behind him made him turn, expecting to see Linda emerging from the bedroom, but the room was empty. He was about to turn away when something attracted his attention. On one of the soiled plates from which he had recently eaten—a fork was sliding backwards and forwards of its own accord!

In utter disbelief Denning watched the pronged end rise an inch, fall back and rise again. Then slowly, as if supported by invisible thread, the fork rose some three feet above the plate, circled twice, then steadied the pronged end pointing straight at his face.

He never knew what prompted him to duck but suddenly the fork leaped at him with the eye-deceiving swiftness of a dragonfly.

There was a dull thud behind him and he had a brief glimpse of the fork sunk two inches into the wall and still quivering like an arrow. Before he could take it in, he was compelled to leap aside for a carving knife which seemed to have come from nowhere and was striking upwards at his stomach.

Unconscious at that moment of unhuman reflexes and

unnatural agility, he crossed the room almost in one stride, grasped a metal service tray and deflected another fork coming straight for his eyes.

The room seemed suddenly full of missiles. A dinner plate struck him painfully on the thigh, a coffee cup broke to fragments on the wall less than an inch from his head and the carpet seemed to writhe up from the floor and almost tripped him.

Desperately he tried to fight back but the tray was suddenly wrenched from his hands and he found himself defenseless.

He dodged another knife, side-stepped the tray which came back at him edgeways, warily keeping his eye on a spiteful-looking pickle fork which was dancing in the air like an angry wasp.

Only faintly did he hear the bedroom door open and sensed rather than saw the brief flashes of crimson light which came from inside.

The pickle fork vanished suddenly in a puff of vapor; the tray, sliding down from the ceiling, crumpled and dissolved into a spray of fragments; a small mat racing towards his legs flared suddenly and became drifting smoke.

Suddenly there was silence and the room was still.

"Are you all right, Richard?" There was genuine concern in Linda's voice.

"I think so. I don't know how—thank you for arriving just in time."

"Thank heaven I did." Slowly, she returned a small gleaming weapon to her purse. "I heard the noise and came running." She looked about the room. "It looks a mess, doesn't it?"

He nodded without speaking. The room was still misted with smoke and the faint but unmistakable tang of ozone, but the place was a shambles. Various utensils were embedded in the walls, the floor was littered with broken crockery, pictures hung askew, one chair had a leg missing and a pane had gone from one of the windows. In the far side wall, presumably due to Linda's weapon, were at least seven blackened holes through which daylight was visible.

Denning rubbed an aching thigh and said, "What now?"

She frowned and shook her head. "I'm sorry, but—well, frankly, from here on, we're on the run." She shook her head again. "I'm at fault. I never realized Kostain would follow up so quickly."

"You mean—?" He stopped, realizing the fatuousness of the question.

"Kostain sent assassins," she said. "They used a manipulator—a sort of radio-control device with an observation screen—so they must be within forty miles. They found us and tried to eliminate us."

"The last part I follow," he said bitterly. "Is there any point in running?"

"They can't have a search beam here with an effective range of more than sixty miles—yes, there's a point in running." Already she was packing. "In point of fact we must run; we're supposed to stay alive until Viegler has us pulled out."

"Thank you for nothing—ever wondered what it feels like to be a classified highly secret weapon?"

"Don't be bitter, Richard, please."

"Why not? Isn't emotional response included in my creation? What the hell else can I be? All I know is that I'm a specialist abstract, the complete enigma who doesn't know what he is or what he is supposed to do and has no control over the situation anyway."

She looked at him and away. Surprisingly, when she answered her voice was low and slightly unsteady. "It's not my fault. I'm only doing a job."

"Yes." His voice was low but vicious. "You're doing an excellent job protecting your superweapon. It just so happens I didn't want to be a superweapon and, furthermore, I strongly resent being treated as a village idiot to whom

59

things must be explained at the proper time." He drew a deep breath. "I'll run with you because I have no choice, but watch it. I might decide that a neat black hole in my head from that nasty little gun of yours is the lesser of two evils. Don't imagine from here on you're going to run things entirely your way because you're an advanced being from a superior technology."

She turned her back on him. "Please, don't say things like that," she said. She laid a pile of notes on the table and became brisk. "That will cover the damage, I imagine—ready?"

"I'm ready." He had not finished but was determined to follow up later. "We'll take my car, it's in the main park. Any objection to me dropping off at my house for some essentials, razor and so on?"

She shook her head, strangely subdued. "You must be quick but, yes, we should have time for that. As soon as I started shooting it probably disrupted their vision beam. They may not be quite sure what happened, and it will take them some forty minutes to refocus."

Less than ten minutes later, he was opening the front door of his house. When he entered the front rom, Marian was lying back in one of the easy chairs.

"I'm just—" He stopped. There was something peculiarly unnatural about her position.

He went closer and felt a sudden coldness in his stomach. Marian was sprawled but arched backwards, her fingers hooked as if she had tried to pull herself upright. An ash tray lay overturned on the floor and a cigarette had burned a hole in the carpet.

On the other side of the table, near the fire place, he found Beacham. The man's arm was still in a sling. A bloody ornamental brass poker lay beside him and the back of his head was battered in.

Denning lit a cigarette, forced himself to inhale deeply, then turned slowly and walked out of the room. He did not look at Marian again, once had been enough—protruding from her throat had been one inch of the handle of a foot-long paper knife which had once lain as an ornament on his desk.

Denning closed the living room door and leaned against it, feeling sweat on his forehead and temples. He did not know if it was his new and logical thinking, but he had the answer almost without reasoning about it. The thought that Marion and Beacham had been murdered by accident, in mistake for Linda and himself, had occurred to him but had been instantly dismissed. Agents from an advanced culture would not make such a clumsy mistake.

No, this was a murder of expedience committed for specific ends. Sooner or later, the bodies would be discovered, the bodies of a married woman and her lover. The police would want the married woman's husband, known to be associating with an auburn-haired woman who had been staying at a nearby hotel—the husband and the woman, however, had disappeared. Not unnaturally, the police would conclude that the husband had killed his wife and her lover and run away with his assumed mistress. In any case, the police would want to interview the husband in a hurry.

Denning brushed sweat from his face. It was all very neat, calculated and quite ruthless. Sooner or later, the police would catch up with him and put him in the nearest prison pending further investigation. The arrest and place of detention would naturally make headlines in the papers. It would be then that a small group of alien agents would move to within forty miles of the prison with an unpleasantly efficient device called a long range manipulator. One morning, no doubt, the prison authorities would find him hanged or with a prison table fork sticking from his throat. There would, of course, be no question—too clearly the verdict would be suicide.

Denning felt a sudden overwhelming hatred for the alien

agents. Very damned smart; there was no need for a chase now. All the assassins needed to do was to sit on their behinds and wait; the native police would do all the chasing for them.

Denning had no illusions concerning the police. They were efficient, highly trained and thorough. Oh, yes, he and Linda could run, would run, switch from car to train, from train to bus, but, in the end, they would be caught. The police would find a certain taxi driver who—a ticket collector who recalled—a barman who remembered serving a man and a woman answering to the description.

Denning closed the front door and ran down to the car. "We've got to run for the nearest town, ditch the car and run again."

He explained quickly what had happened as they drove, conscious that they must get rid of the car as soon as possible.

They made the next big town in thirty minutes, abandoned the car in one of the big car parks and caught a taxi to the Central Hotel. Once the taxi had departed, they flagged down another and were driven to the nearest station. Here they took a local to another station and this time Denning booked long distance.

The car was occupied by two middle-aged ladies and a youth with a transistor radio. As the train pulled out of the station, the pop music stopped suddenly. *"Here is a police message in connection with a double murder believed to have taken place in the early hours of this morning. The police are anxious to contact a man who they believe can help them in their inquiries. Here is name and description. He is Richard Denning, age——"*

At this point, the youth switched to another station and the rest of the message was lost.

Denning shifted his feet slightly and hoped the sweat on his face had passed unnoticed. They would have to think of something fast.

62

An hour later, the train stopped at an intermediate station and they quietly left the train. The stop proved to be a small rural town and a tired-looking man accepted their tickets without bothering to check them.

Ten minutes later, they were on the outskirts of the town and heading down a winding country lane.

"Where are we going?" Linda made the question almost gay. She seemed singularly untroubled.

He scowled, irritated by her mood. "God knows. Trying for a room without luggage would be asking for arrest. No doubt my picture has graced nearly every television screen in the country by now."

"There's a hay stack over there." She pointed.

He snarled at her. "What the hell do you think this is— a camping holiday?"

"You'd prefer to walk all night, perhaps? It's getting dark, and at least it's a place to rest. I had the foresight to bring some sandwiches too, remember? We could sit down and eat them and, perhaps, decide our next move."

"We could also light a small fire," he said, bitterly. "The police could then brew some tea when they catch up with us, which, in my opinion, will be too damned soon for comfort."

"Don't be such a pessimist, Richard. If things get too rough, Veigler will have us pulled out."

"That's all right for you." He lowered himself angrily into the deep straw. "For me, it's just being hauled out of the frying pan and into the fire."

She sat down beside him. "Do you think I want to go back? Do you know what it was like to come here and see trees? Do you know what it's like to see the sun, watch it move across the sky, smell flowers, hear birds singing when all you've ever seen is ice and a line of fire on the horizon?"

"And that," he said, "is your alternative to arrest. Very nice. Once there, presumably, I shall be handed over to the authorities for operations against the enemy."

She leaned towards him, then drew back. "It's no good saying I'm sorry, no good telling you it's not my fault." She turned her head away and when she spoke again her voice was strangely muffled. "I know how you feel, but you don't want me."

He said, savagely. "When I want a woman giving herself in line of duty I'll let you know. Your intelligence people will no doubt be delighted that their weapon behaved according to plan and you, yourself, can write 'mission accomplished' at the bottom of the official report."

She turned on him and, in the gathering darkness, he was shocked to see her eyes filled with tears. "You rat, you earth-thing." Her voice broke. At that moment she was wholly woman and no longer an assured agent from an advanced culture. "How stupid can a man get? I told you I volunteered. You were no stranger—I'd monitored your life for several years, watched you from Firma. Oh God, do I have to draw a diagram?"

"So you watched me, you volunteered. What does that prove? Only that you're a conscientious agent."

"You're cruel, Richard, cruel." She was trying desperately to regain her composure and failing hopelessly. "I've tried so hard, so damned hard, but—" Her voice broke suddenly and she was silent.

Realization and inescapable guilt dawned on him at the same moment. He was like a hurt child striking at anything within distance, blindly and without reason. He was petty, cruel, narrow—why had she volunteered? After all, her main job was to guard him and, after he had rejected her offer, she could have bowed out gracefully. But she had continued to—*Oh, God, do I have to draw a diagram?*

With a mixture of elation and despair he realized at that moment that she was in love with him. Now, he'd messed everything up. Was it too late? Could he make her understand?

He turned towards her, laid his hand on her shoulder

and felt her body shaking with sobs. "Linda, I'm sorry, I didn't understand, I didn't *know*."

She jerked her body away. "Go to hell." She sounded choked.

"Now, look, just let me explain." He put his hand on her shoulder again and pulled her gently, forgetting his strength.

Suddenly she was close.

"Get away from me."

"No, Linda, please." He held her.

"Get away, don't touch me, fight me—I can't—you can't —oh God—" Her arms went round his neck. "I can't fight you."

"Why the hell couldn't you say—" he began and realized suddenly how close she was. It was then he forgot everything. . . .

Denning was never sure later if he slept and, sleeping, woke and slept again, or if he experienced a kind of waking dream.

It seemed that one moment he was lying at peace in the hay and the next the world exploded slowly in an expanding kaleidoscope of changing light and fire.

In his dream, he called for Linda but she did not answer; he tried to touch her, but she was not there. Tears filled his eyes. He struggled desperately but was carried away on a wave of darkness into a curious limbo of paleness which was palpable and pressed against him like jelly.

He was conscious but unable to move. Strange cubes and rectangles of color drifted past his eyes, ponderously, meditatively, like sleepy fish in a still lake.

He became slowly aware that something was with him. Something half-seen from the corner of his eye which, when he shifted his gaze, was no longer there.

Chapter Seven

He was surprised to find he was not afraid. The thing, whatever it was, seemed to be pouring assurance into his mind, assurance, understanding compassion.

It was like a doctor or a nurse, soothing, explaining, rectifying and, there was no doubt about it, agreeing with Denning's own sense of injustice. No, he had not deserved it, yes, much was unnecessary, it would be corrected—later —later——

The paleness slowly vanished and he was swept away again, carried high on the crest of an unseen wave and flung heavily on the rocky shore.

For a long time he was incapable of movement. Wave after wave of nausea enveloped and re-enveloped him. He seemed to be swinging, lurching, yawing and he tried to cling to the flat rock desperately with his fingers.

Strangely his mind was clear and he *knew*. He knew precisely what had happened and how frantic both parties must be knowing that——

The Lollies, the people Linda represented, had been following events with a sub-continuum monitoring device and, seeing that conditions on Earth were becoming precarious, had decided to pull them out.

Unfortunately, the opposition, wearying of the pedestrian slowness of the native police, decided on an experiment of their own. Could the fugitives be pulled out and into a Co-temp laboratory with their own instruments? They decided to try.

Both parties knew of and could apply the Brethanger principles, but in each case the modus operandi varied slightly. It was, however, a frightening coincidence that both parties set their mechanisms working at precisely the same moment.

The result was that he, Denning, had received a double application of power which had hurled him through the repetitive cycle into an exterior or wholly variable cycle.

An alien intelligence, both compassionate and acutely aware of the law of repetitive reflections, had done its best to correct the error and returned him, it hoped, more or less to his own cycle.

In the meantime, both parties were checking their equipment frantically, fully alive to the fact that they had lost him. In due course, precise checking would enable them to triangulate his position to within two or three light years—that is, of course, if Denning still existed as a corporeal being.

Denning shifted slightly, fought down an urge to retch and continued to think. He knew what he was, he knew by mental application he could adjust his metabolic rate to extremes of heat and cold. He knew he was abnormally strong, a precise thinking instrument and, most important of all, the reasons for his driving sex urges.

He found also that many misconceptions and inhibitions due to upbringing had disappeared and that he was now far more capable of surviving in an environment which, even with his powers, might have placed him at a disadvantage.

The nausea began to recede slowly and he made cautious exploratory movements with his hands. The surface beneath him should have been hay, but he knew it wasn't. It felt like rock and was warm to the touch as if exposed to the sun.

Carefully he opened his eyes but his vision swam, forcing him to close them again. He had, however, managed to get an impression of water sparkling in the sunlight—the sea shore? Where? Must be Earth, couldn't be Firma; according to Linda, there were no oceans on Firma.

He opened his eyes again and this time the scene steadied. He was looking at a small artificial pond in which swam myriads of tiny scarlet fish. Huge flowers, like inflated purple water lilies, lay on the surface surrounded by flat oily-looking pink and white leaves.

A fountain played in the middle of the pond, dividing into numerous smaller jets at its apex so that it, too, looked like a strange shimmering plant.

He raised his head slightly, retched, but fought down the nausea. There was a wide green lawn, neatly clipped hedges, a group of small trees—an improbable mixture of dwarf pine, palm and willow—and what looked like a small gaily painted summer house.

After a few minutes he was able to stagger to his feet. Above him a late afternoon sun shone from a cloudless sky across which black dots, presumably birds, raced at incredible speed as if carried by tremendous winds. Down here, however, was only a gentle breeze.

He walked across the lawn, passed through an opening in the neatly clipped hedge and stopped. In front of him was a low wall, and beyond the wall the roofs and buildings of a city stretched into endless distance.

This was not then, as he had imagined, the grounds of a country estate, but a roof garden on the top of a huge but curiously squat building.

Directly below him was a street packed with racing, pear-shaped vehicles without wheels, held by some unknown force some nine inches above the surface of the road.

The vehicles seemed to Denning peculiarly garish and reminded him strongly of a fun fair. All were brightly painted, many of them striped or checkered in glaring variations. All bore an overabundance of shining metal resembling chromium which was arranged into various shapes like jet tubes, stubby wings or even ancient exhaust pipes.

Several feet above the level of the traffic and on each side of the street was a moving pathway. It was packed with pedestrians in bright pastel clothing who were being carried swiftly along the seemingly endless street. The complementary pavement across the highway, he noticed, moved swiftly in the opposite direction.

Denning ran his practiced architect's eye over the buildings. All were squat and, although "dressed" and cleverly colored to give an impression of height and line, reminded him strongly of flat-topped pyramids.

It struck him suddenly that the construction was functional, and he experienced a cold sensation in his stomach. All these buildings, judging by their construction, rested on an individual apron of metal or similar durable substances. In the event of an upheaval, such as a major earthquake, they were almost indestructible. He looked closer. Yes, the buildings, unless he was very much mistaken, were deliberately stressed to take punishment. Access, too, he noticed, was by self-sealing solid looking doors, reached by broad steps, some ten feet above ground level.

Denning no longer wondered where he was—he knew. This was the Co-temp zone of Firma.

The alien had returned him safely, but had almost literally deposited him into the arms of the people most anxious to dispose of him.

"Who, in the name of Sin, are you?" said a voice behind him.

He jumped and spun round so quickly he almost lost his balance.

A man stood behind him. A tall man with exquisitely waved hair, he was fair and striking, though he possessed slightly battered classical features. He wore a shimmering blue robe, belted at the waist, which looked like a cross between a dressing gown and a toga.

"Well, I am waiting." The large, almost feminine, blue eyes looked into Denning's arrogantly and with a hint of challenge.

"I—" Denning spread his hands helplessly, realizing he had no plausible explanation. "I'm here—I'm sorry."

"You are here, yes, but you have not, as yet, begun to be sorry." The man looked him up and down speculatively. "Clearly, in that archaic costume you are a member of one of the cults. Presumably you dropped from a private flyer on some hare-brained scheme or with a view to robbery, but you picked the wrong house." He paused and stroked his chin thoughtfully. "You are a nice size, almost the right size."

Again he paused, pursing his lips. "I have a mind to take you apart, piece by piece, here and now." He made an abrupt gesture with his right hand, and the lower half of Denning's body became suddenly cold and immovable.

"In case you don't understand what has happened, dear boy, that little gesture of mine was received by an electronic device, which in turn activated a nerve-freeze unit. As you will have gathered, I am not unprepared for the unlawful intruder." He stepped forward. "I propose keeping it on until I have searched you thoroughly."

He began a thorough search of Denning's clothing with a delighted running commentary. "But how thorough you are. This antique lighter must have cost a pretty sum—ah, ball pens, how quaint, kerchief, key ring, packaged cigarettes, well, really."

Finally, he finished. "At least you are unarmed." He made another gesture.

The coldness receded from Denning's body and was replaced with an excruciating pain.

"Painful, isn't it? It doesn't last, however." The man

smiled again. "Tell me what you are doing here. I don't expect the truth, but one can hope—well?"

Denning shrugged. "I wanted money and a change of clothing."

"I see." The other nodded thoughtfully. "Perhaps my hopes of frankness are rewarded, but that is not all, is it? You have an unnatural pallor, you speak with an obscure but audible accent, but you are well fed and outwardly healthy. Your intent to rob, therefore, was not inspired by gain alone—to procure some essential drug or the demands of a perversion—but for more primitive reasons. It occurs to me, therefore, you are on the run, either from authority or the vengeance of a rival cult. Your need for money, therefore, is for bribes, transit, a hide-out."

Denning resisted a temptation to move uncomfortably. The man was getting too close for comfort.

"Ah, so I am not too far from the target, eh? I see it in your face." The other nodded quickly. "You are surprised, perhaps, that I am so astute, but I am all surprises. In this day and age, in this jungle of ignorance, decay and violence, I hold degrees in social logistics, in general philosophy, in applied psychology. It is true, of course, that such degrees bring in no money and carry no recognition or honor, but they had to be *earned*. I earned them. If nothing else, I showed this zone that a man can rise above the decadence of his environment. I prove, each day, the truth of the maxim *mens sana in corpore sano.*"

He paused, and again he looked at Denning speculatively. "It is clear from your face that you do not know me and, perhaps, you have never heard of me, but professionally I am known as Marko. It is a name well known in the arenas of the zone, for I have fought in them all. I have boxed in metal gauntlets, stabbed with short sword and trident, traded blows with clubs and axes. Ah, yes, the days of ancient Roma are not forgotten; people pay high money for blood sports, particularly when it is human blood

71

and their own is not endangered. Always it is the same. When a civilization begins to decay, the blood sports come back—the mutilation is a release from boredom."

Marko sighed and looked at Denning speculatively again. "You appreciate, I hope, that it is my duty to hand you over to the authorities? On the other hand, I am a sportsman, and we have here no blood-crazed mob to turn down the thumb and scream for a death blow. I'll make you a proposition. I will give you a thousand notes and a change of clothing in return for certain services. If you, too, are a sportsman the proposition may appeal to you. If not, then, alas, I must do my duty by the zone and refer you to the police."

Denning said, bitterly, "I don't seem to have much choice —what is this proposition?"

Marko smiled. "I will be frank, dear boy. I am a champion, I have killed more men in the arena than I care to think about. In consequence, despite the high wages I offer, practice opponents are hard to come by, even when offered the inducements of protective clothing and expert medical attention. I am, therefore, offering you the position in exchange for your freedom. No—wait. Never let it be said that Marko was ungenerous. If you can stand up to me for five minutes only, I will make it two thousand notes."

"Only there will be no protective clothing?"

"My dear fellow, I am a sportsman, not a philanthropist. On the face of it I consider my offer generous in the extreme."

"Assuming I'm around to collect?"

"You have a sporting chance, dear boy, a sporting chance." He undid the robe and let it fall to the ground. "If you would care to follow me, I have a gymnasium and a small arena in which I practice."

Denning stared and swallowed, feeling a tightness in his throat. Beneath the robe Marko wore only mock-leopard-skin tights, and the man was built like a god. Beneath the lightly tanned skin, the huge muscles rippled and moved as if they possessed life of their own. The chest and shoulders were gigantic, yet despite this the man was beautifully proportioned. He looked what he was, a physical superman, and there was in his expression, at that moment, something else—Marko was a killer.

"I am waiting, my friend."

Denning swallowed again, trying to relieve the dryness in his throat. At first he had had hopes that superior strength might prevail but, after seeing the man, he very much doubted if his strength was superior. Secondly, Marko was experienced and he, Denning, knew literally nothing about fighting of any kind.

He sighed. "Very well, I can delude myself I have a fighting chance. In the hands of the authorities I should be denied that delusion."

Marko bowed slightly. "A sportsman's choice, dear boy. I salute your decision." He turned. "This way—oh, and yes, I forgot the formalities. It is only fitting that you should decide the weapons. What shall it be—short swords, net and trident, clubs? I advise against clubs; they are extraordinarily unwieldly for a beginner."

Denning said bitterly, "Thank you for your concern but, if it's all the same to you, I'd prefer bare hands."

"Ah, now." Marko shook his head sadly. "I was afraid you were going to say that. It is a mistake made by all tyros; they imagine they are safer when facing an opponent without weapons. Tell me, do you know how many ways there are to kill a man with the bare hands?"

"No, and I don't damned well want to," said Denning, suddenly angry. "I've no doubt you'll demonstrate most of them before you administer the *coup de grâce*."

"Hush, dear boy, do not lose your temper. A hot head in the arena is a virtual invitation to defeat."

"Blast you," Denning said savagely and fought down a

73

temptation to leap at him then and there. The man was not only relishing the coming fight, but he was adding insult to injury by downright patronage.

Marko led the way, via a short moving stairway, to a huge, brightly lit gumnasium. In the center was a circular depression reminding Denning strongly of a circus ring.

"You may change in there." Marko indicated a cubicle. "It is fully equipped but all you will need are the tights."

When Denning emerged some seconds later, he felt naked and a little cold and had an inclination to hug himself like an indifferent swimmer approaching a cold and very rough sea.

Marko stood waiting in the ring, unconsciously posing and flexing the magnificent muscles pointedly.

Denning fought down a desire to turn and run and stepped into the ring.

Marko smiled at him. "Salute the challenger." The smile, however, lacked geniality and the blue eyes were cold and appraising. "Not bad, at least you are not all string and tendon; nonetheless, I propose taking you apart piece by piece. Have you any relatives to whom your wages may be forwarded?"

Denning said, "No," and "Go to hell," all in one breath. He was acutely alive to the fact that not only was he terrified but that Marko knew it.

"Shall we begin, dear boy?" Very deliberately Marko put his hands behind his back. "I'll make it easy—come in and take me."

Denning stood still. He had no experience but it looked too easy for comfort. It was one thing to suspect a noose, quite another to stick his head in to find out.

"Go to hell," he said and dropped into what he hoped was a wrestlers pose.

"Have it your way, dear boy." Marko was on him before he knew it with a speed and coordination of movement which was literally terrifying.

74

He felt one hand slap and grasp his wrist, the other strike the side of his head with a force which made his ears sing. Then, his right arm felt as if it was being twisted out of its socket and pain forced him to his knees.

"Piece by piece, dear boy," said Marko, softly. "Piece by piece." His other hand came down on the back of Denning's neck, forcing his face to the floor. Marko banged it several times forcibly on the floor of the arena before changing his tactics and lifting the other completely from the floor.

It seemed to Denning that the gymnasium was suddenly moving around him, and he realized abruptly that he was being held like a toy at arm's length above Marko's head while he spun round on his toes.

Desperately, and becoming increasingly dizzy, he groped for a hand to hold but it was hopeless—he was being spun round like a top.

Suddenly Marko threw him. Denning sailed dizzily through the air, but instinctively rolled himself into a ball, thus saving himself broken bones. Even so, he landed so heavily that most of the breath was knocked from his body.

He lay still, gasping.

"Get up, my little plaything, get up." Marko stood over him menacingly.

Denning sucked in air desperately. Marko, he realized, was just as much a part of the decadent society he claimed to have risen above as any one else in the zone. In short, he was a sadist. Not only was he relishing every second of mutilating a nearly defenseless opponent, but he was deliberately taking his time. He could have killed within the first few seconds, but that would have denied him the pleasures of his perversion. He intended, as he had stated, to take Denning apart piece by piece, but he was determined to inflict the maximum amount of agony doing so.

Shakily, he climbed to his feet. Marko promptly knocked

him down with a heavy although obviously "pulled" blow to his face.

This time, however, Denning pretended to be only partly conscious; he had to have time to think. It was clear, unless a miracle occurred or he pulled something unforeseen out of the hat, the situation was desperate. The trouble was, he realized, that he had never really *believed* that Marko intended to kill him—God, he had to do *something* fast.

Chapter Eight

"Get up, my little friend." Marko's voice was soft and almost inviting. "I shall count up to ten and, if you are not up by then, I shall be compelled to tear off your left ear."

Denning was conscious of goose pimples covering his entire body but his mind was detached, cold and working factually. He had to keep clear of this man somehow, stop him coming to grips.

Suddenly he stiffened, rolled desperately away from Marko and sprang to his feet.

"Oh, ho!" Marko looked almost pleased. "We have spirit! This makes my day."

Denning said nothing, but desperately assumed the pose of boxers he had seen on television. Perhaps Marko had not studied boxing.

Marko had. He showed his perfect teeth briefly and danced on his toes. Then he came in, bobbing and weaving.

Denning pushed out a fast but none too well-timed left. Marko saw it coming and covered expertly, taking the blow on his forearm.

There was a muffled snapping noise and Denning felt pain shoot up his hand, but Marko staggered backwards, his face mirroring pain and utter disbelief.

Denning slung a wild right hook. Marko rode the blow skillfully, avoiding most of its force, but even so he toppled sideways as if he had been pole-axed.

Denning jumped on him before he could recover and got his forearm across the other's throat. "Give in or I'll pull your damned head off."

Marko beat a limp hand on the ground. Clearly he was

dazed; equally clearly he was already choking to death. His eyes bulged and his tongue protruded between his teeth.

Denning eased his hold but was ready for any sudden counter move.

Marko gasped, choked and wheezed desperately for breath for what seemed an extraordinarily long time, then he spat out a broken tooth. "I give in—it—it—is your decision."

Denning stood back, and the other struggled to his knees, shaking his head dazedly. "You could have killed me. Mother of God, you could have killed *me*—who are you?"

"Does it matter?"

"Not now—if you will help me to the medical room, please. It's the green door over there."

In the medical room, Marko dropped heavily into the nearest chair and sprayed his face with a greenish liquid which seemed to vanish instantly into the pores of the skin. One side of his face was swollen and badly bruised.

Next he swallowed a small yellow pill and almost instantly became outwardly his old self. "I shall need medical aid later, but the pain is gone. You appreciate, I hope, that you have fractured my forearm, torn a muscle in my shoulder and, I suspect, broken a bone in my cheek—you are not human, are you?"

Denning shrugged. "Is it important?"

"Only to my pride. I must assure myself that I have not been beaten by a normal man, particularly one whose knowledge of self-defense is less than elementary. My God, my dear fellow, you hadn't a chance. You were as wide as a barn, but you conquered me by sheer strength—reassure me for pity's sake."

Denning sighed. "Shall we say I come from very far away?"

"Enough, enough!" Marko raised one of his huge hands. "You are a stranger here; I sensed that from the first, but

I am in no position to ask impertinent questions. In the first place I owe you your wages, and in the second I owe you a debt which I cannot repay. You could have killed me—in your position I would have killed you—but you let me live." He frowned, obviously sincere. "I am a sportsman, a life for a life—if you are in danger, come to me and I will repay."

He paused and looked at the other directly. "After which, of course, I reserve the rights of combat. I shall be swift and final next time."

"You have a peculiar chivalry."

"Perhaps, but let us be grateful it survives among sportsmen." He stroked his injured arm thoughtfully. "Of broken bones and torn muscles I make no complaint. These things are honorable scars, the medals of combat. I have had them before, but never from a single man with two wild and untrained blows."

He swallowed another yellow pill. "So you are a stranger here—how much do you know of this zone?"

"Literally nothing."

Marko clicked his tongue disapprovingly. "I will give you money and clothes, but without prior instruction your chance of survival is small." He paused. "When I first came upon you, you were looking down into the city—shall I tell you what you were really looking at, dear boy? You were looking down at a jungle such as never existed in the entire history of this planet. A jungle which is fiercer, more violent and far more subtle and insidious than any which graced the swamps when the dinosaur was king. It will embrace you like a beautiful woman and slit your throat with a jagged knife before you can drink from its lips. Listen—"

Denning listened while Marko prepared him for life, or at least possible survival, in the zone. He explained the monetary system, how to use the elevators and the moving ways. He told Denning where to go and where not to go, and he did his best to warn of the dangers.

"This city will offer you drugs for a handful of notes, which will transport you to a dream world where you are God. Drugs which create worlds of your own choosing, drugs which, even if you are in your dotage, would run you through a gamut of sexual excesses which you could never hope to experience at the peak of your virility."

He paused and shook his head sadly. "They call these drugs non-habit-forming, which physically is true but which psychologically bind one forever. Every day one meets the dreamers—the living dead who cannot distinguish between the dream and the reality."

He smiled at Denning twistedly. "These are but a few of the burdens of privilege, the chosen who sew not, neither do they spin but who, nonetheless, must find an answer to the everlasting boredom of absolute leisure." Marko laughed abruptly. "Words carry me away for I, too, deceive myself. Behold, I am king of the jungle but, nonetheless, its victim."

He rose. "Come, I am demoralizing my own ego—you need clothes and money."

In the next room he found Denning a smart lightweight suit which he handed to him with a flourish. "The best money can buy, dear boy, eight hundred and sixty notes and I've never worn it. Can't stand pink, don't really know why I bought it."

Denning put it on. It looked several sizes too large but adapted instantly to his size as soon as he slipped on the jacket.

"Ah, yes, money." Marko pushed a pile of plastic squares into his hand which reminded him strongly of playing cards. "There's five thousand there, more than double my promise. I am sorry I had to pay you in fifties but I never bother with oncers, too plebian, too reminiscent of governmental standard allowances, you understand." He frowned slightly. "Are you sure you remember all I have told you—hotel costs, traffic regulations, police checks and so on?"

"Yes, thank you." Denning was surprised to find he could repeat it word for word. He seemed, among other things, to have acquired a startlingly retentive memory.

"Well, good luck, dear boy." Marko held out his un-injured hand. "Don't forget, I am still in your debt."

Seconds later, Denning found himself descending by an elevator which resembled an ornately furnished room and gave no sense of motion whatever. Only when an exquisite mural slid to one side did he realize that he had reached the street.

He stepped forward and hesitated. There was, as Marko had told him, a green "on" sign just in front of the door; but although it said "on," it omitted to say "how."

The moving sidewalk was, in no sense, pedestrian, and he estimated that its passengers were being carried past him at twenty to thirty miles an hour. The idea of simply stepping on it, packed as it was, at that speed was anything but attractive.

At that moment an elderly woman stepped calmly in front of him, walked over the green "on" sign and was suddenly swept away with the rest, apparently unharmed and obviously unruffled.

Denning scowled, feeling rather like a nervous schoolboy afraid to venture even into shallow water. Well, if an old lady could do it, surely to God he could follow.

He stepped forward, acutely aware that his expression must be that of an initiate ordered to walk the plank, but hoping desperately it was all the joking part of the ceremony.

As he stepped forward, invisible forces seemed to press against the soles of his feet while other forces steadied him by the shoulders, and then his feet were planted firmly on the moving way and he was carried swiftly but without vertigo away with the others.

He was surprised to find there was no stiff breeze such as might be expected at over twenty miles an hour, nor, apart from visual observation, was there any sense of motion. One knew, if one looked, that one was moving swiftly along the street but on closing the eyes one might well be standing still.

Denning shrugged it off wonderingly and began to study the people about him. The men wore bright but pastel suits of various colors like his own, but the women, particularly the younger ones, caused him to flush and avert his eyes hastily. The fashion was to picture hats, tight bodices and voluminous skirts, but both bodice and skirt, although of varying colors, were absolutely and wholly transparent.

He turned his attention to the street, which at first seemed very little different from the streets of his own planet in his own time. There were numerous stores with invisible glass, colored although far more garish, advertising signs, eating houses, and varied, if dubious, places of entertainment.

It took him some minutes to realize that although it *looked* much the same the content was different. There were, of course, familiar things; the usual visual inducements to purchase patent medicines, liquor, food, insurance, and cars, but there were other advertisements. . . .

In smoky pink lettering spanning the entire street was an invitation to all and sundry to visit what was clearly a house of ill repute. Beneath, in smaller lettering, was a long list of perversions and variations which, the advertisement assured him, could be secured for only two and one half per cent extra.

On an opposite building an undulating caterpillar of green words said: GET DRUGGED! GET AWAY FROM THE WORLD! RIDE A DREAM OF YOUR OWN CHOOSING! ANY TASTE CATERED FOR IN PRECISE DETAIL! ALL OUR COMPOUNDS GUARANTEED NON-HABIT-FORMING.

And, less than a hundred feet farther on: BECOME

A SATANIST! OBSCENE RITES AT EVERY SER-
VICE.

Denning closed his eyes briefly and wondered if he was dreaming. When he opened them again a blue pillar of words invited him to own his own harem: SYNTHETIC WOMEN! ALMOST IMPOSSIBLE TO DISTINGUISH FROM THE GENUINE ARTICLE! OBEDIENT, PAS-SIONATE AND CHEAP TO MAINTAIN!

He looked wildly about him for a way of escape. He was beginning to understand what Marko had meant by a decaying jungle. Then, close to a pyramid of blue letters advertising advanced sadism, he saw the one small word, PARK.

He waited for an 'off' sign and stepped off the band. Once again his feet and ankles were gripped by an invisible force, once again his shoulders were steadied and he was held erect. There was no jerk and no feeling of nausea.

He passed through a small ornamental gate and was surprised to find himself in a genuine park. He suspected that the thrush singing its heart out in a thicket was a recording and the procession of swans on the small lake seemed too regular and precise in their careful circling to be real, but the rest was wholly normal. The grass was real grass, the flowers exotic but living and the trees draping their tresses in the water were real willows.

He found a seat beneath a tree and sat down feeling a little dazed. How many days ago was it since he had been driving his comfortable, familiar Ford on Earth, not dreaming——

He frowned, forcing himself to think constructively. He was *here*. He had enough money, living frugally, to live here eighteen months, but after that—what? Clearly his hopes of leaving the zone undetected, let alone alive, were negligible. According to his information, it was just as hard to get out as it was to get in and, even if he succeeded, what had he gained? How many miles would he have to travel before he met those directly responsible for his well-being? Again, for all he knew, they had given him up for dead. If not, it was up to them to put up some sort of rescue effort—assuming, of course, he was as special as they said he was. He felt a sudden overwhelming ache for Linda and pushed her memory hastily out of his mind. God, he hoped and prayed she was safe, but he could not afford a divided mind now. His immediate concern was to remain alive and undetected.

He recalled what he had seen and shivered slightly. Truly, it was a jungle and—let's face it—he was singularly ill-equipped to survive in it.

His only advantage, if it was an advantage, was that he understood the social and cultural implications behind it. Here was a privileged society groaning under the stress of absolute leisure and frantically seeking escape not only from boredom but from a completely aimless existence. To compensate, countless "escape" entertainments had come into existence under conditions which made the enforcement of moralities impossible. Only the purveyors of such mechanisms had aim: the accumulation of wealth and power, regardless.

In such a society, however, his hopes of remaining undetected were heightened. People didn't *care*. If there were busybodies and nosey parkers, they were too small a minority to worry about. This was a rat race after pleasure and escape; very few were going to bother about one man, and the possible danger of his existence would get home to only a few.

Denning made a mental grimace. "Privileged Class" was a relative phrase, wasn't it?

"Attention!"

He jumped. The word seemed to come from someone invisible standing directly in front of him. A quick look around, however, informed him that others in the park had also heard the word, and he correctly concluded that some sort of oral beaming device was in operation.

"Attention! This is the Ministry of Internal Security calling the entire zone on an emergency hook-up." The voice paused, then continued. *"Attention all Bounty Hunters! Attention all citizens! Hue and Cry!—Repeat—Hue and Cry! A subversive and suspected saboteur from one of the underprivileged areas is at loose in the zone. Here is his description:*

Denning, feeling cold inside, heard himself described in complete and accurate detail.

"Information in possession of the Ministry suggests that this agent is armed and dangerous. Citizens, therefore, should make no effort to apprehend this man themselves but should report immediately to the police guardian service or the nearest Bounty Hunter.

"In view of the urgency of this matter, the Ministry guarantees the sum of thirty thousand notes for the destruction or arrest of this agent and five thousand notes to any citizen for information leading to said destruction or arrest. Further bulletins and any additional information regarding this agent will be broadcast at intervals of one hour.

Denning's first thought was to rise from the chair and get out of the park as quickly as possible, but he checked himself. The Ministry would not have put out a message like that if they knew where he was. It was clear they knew he was somewhere in the zone but they had no idea where.

If he rose now it might attract attention and, furthermore, at the far end of the pseudo-gravel path were two uniformed figures. He had seen them coming a few seconds before the broadcast and to move now would arouse instant suspicion.

Instead of rising, Denning feigned sleep and watched

the approaching men from under half-closed eyes. It was clear that the two were police; they wore round helmets like the Z.P. Their uniforms, however, were bright blue and might have been smart save for an overabundance of scarlet piping.

Watching them approach and draw level, Denning found them repellent. Their faces seemed carved into masks of alert benevolence as if they were striving constantly to look like guardians of the people, but their eyes were never still—cold penetrating eyes which flickered and darted from side to side like the tongues of venomous snakes.

The same eyes flickered over him, assessed him, flickered back and away and then the two were past.

He waited until the two passed through the gate, then breathed an inward sigh of relief and left by another exit.

Outside, he jumped the moving way once more. This time he no longer looked at the outward signs of decay but at the people about him. He was alert for the suspicious face, the look of recognition, the determined but stealthy approach of what might be an agent of the secret police.

After traveling about two miles, he saw something on the opposite side of the highway which instantly alerted him.

It was a man in a bright green suit who stood at the side of the moving way watching the passengers with bright, alert eyes. The man wore a curious Tyrolean kind of hat with a high bright feather and carried something beneath his arm strongly resembling a high-powered rifle. Slung over his left shoulder by a strap was a small black box which reminded Denning strongly of a Geiger counter. Periodically the man consulted the box, then studied the people passing him as if expecting some reaction.

Denning felt suddenly cold, friendless and hunted. Clearly the man was not searching for radioactive ores, but something else. The black box, therefore, was some sort of detector which, when it reacted, told the man in green exactly where to point the long-barreled weapon which looked like a rifle. This man, then, was what the broadcast had described as a Bounty Hunter.

Chapter Nine

Denning was a little vague as to the origin of the term on Earth, but he knew what it meant on this world. Here was a man—possibly a large number of men—out to kill him for the reward. They were, no doubt, trained killers, natural born hunters, skilled in their task, enjoying it and appropriately licensed by the authorities.

He stepped quickly off the way at the nearest "off" sign and looked quickly around for some sort of cover. He was quite certain that the men in green had posted themselves at regular intervals along all major highways with a skill born of long experience.

He did not know if the Geigerlike detectors could work through walls, but he hoped not. His best bet, then, was some small cafe with two exits.

He saw a sign which said: COFFEE AND PULSE BAR. He shouldered his way through the swing door and realized too late that it was not quite what he had expected.

Inside it was almost dark, and there were a number of small tables complete with chairs set round a larger table upon which was a thing which looked like an enlarged version of the crystal ball used by fortune tellers. The ball emitted a curious, steadily pulsating pink radiance, although inside it was a shifting spectrum of changing color.

There was a small group of both sexes in the room, and he saw instantly they were teenagers. They were, however, so grotesque in dress and appearance they seemed barely human.

The faces of the youths were unnaturally white, as if coated with gloss paint. Their heads were completely shaved save for a small greasy pigtail about four inches long which hung from the back of the skull. They wore brightly colored, heavily embroidered waistcoats like gauchos, which left their thin white arms bare.

Below the waistcoats, they wore brightly colored full-length tights, such as those worn by male ballet dancers. Round the waist was a wide shiny belt jingling with—he thought at first glance—trinkets and ornaments.

The girls wore similar clothing, but their hair was frizzed upwards into an elaborate point which resembled a witch's hat. Their makeup, too, was equally bizarre and was apparently composed of metallic compounds, so that their faces appeared sardonic metal masks. There was one girl with golden eyelids and golden lips who resembled a thin-faced and emasculated Buddha.

He took a chair with its back to the wall, dialed the "servo" for coffee and decided to sit it out for at least a few minutes while he figured out what to do next.

The teenagers, however, distracted his attention. It was clear they spoke a wholly incomprehensible language and had a set of manners and customs all their own.

At first, he had dismissed them as a group of extremists similar to the gangs and beatniks back on Earth, but he now had the feeling that this went a little deeper.

Periodically members of the group sniffed at small tubes which, he suspected, contained drugs, and they seemed obsessed with the crystal ball as if deriving some sensual or esoteric pleasure from the pulsating pink light.

Again, they seemed unaware of his intrusion and had not glanced in his direction.

Too late he realized that the group had formed a half-circle about his table, effectively barring his way of escape.

Tense, he watched one of the youths detach himself from the others and approach his table.

"What here, creep-tube?" He was an unpleasant-looking youth with a high, thin forehead and little glassy blue eyes.

Denning stared at him blankly. "I'm sorry, I don't understand you."

"You're a tube, a flow-through, catchee feller-boy? You don't ride the pulse—compree?"

One of the girls came forward, a silver mask, sardonic. Her finger nails were polished to match the face and looked like talons. Like the boys she wore the same open waistcoat, and she did not seem to care if it fell open.

Denning noticed that she was slenderly and beautifully built, and there was something in her eyes which suggested he interested her.

"Non compree, Carlos." She said to Denning. "Carlos says you're a tube. In short, you're incapable of reacting to the subtleties of the pulse. It flows through you, does not stimulate, hence a tube—plain?"

"Plain, but is that my fault?"

"Feller-boy creep-tube," said Carlos.

"He thinks you're anti-pulse," the girl translated.

"Really!" Denning was suddenly angry. "Well, you tell Carlos I don't know what a pulse is. I just dropped in for coffee and, when I'm permitted, I'll leave."

"Pigeon talk," said Carlos. He fingered his belt meaningfully and Denning saw that what he had taken for trinkets were really miniature but precisely fashioned weapons. Inch-long exquisite daggers, barbs, tomahawks and a tiny weapon resembling an automatic pistol which was no bigger than a penny. They did not look like dangerous weapons, but it was abundantly clear that Carlos was not fingering them for amusement.

"Carlos does not believe you," obliged the girl.

Denning shrugged. "So?"

"Pulse check," said Carlos. He turned. "Who's riding it?"

"I ride," said a wizened-looking youth with a ginger pigtail.

"We'll check you through the pulse," the girl said to

Denning. "For your sake, I hope you're positive—Carlos is aching to chop you."

A chair was dragged forward and the ginger youth sank into it, fixing Denning with pale, watery-blue eyes.

There was a sudden silence, and the pulsating pink light from the crystal ball seemed to increase in tempo and become almost palpable. For the first time, Denning became aware of a strange sub-audible rhythm which seemed to sing inside his head.

The pale eyes of the youth in the chair seemed suddenly to go blank and his body stiffened.

"He's carried." It was a whisper.

Sweat broke out on the youth's forehead, and there was an audible gasp. "He exudes!"

It appeared to Denning that they looked at the youth and at himself with a certain awe.

The thin body arched backwards in the chair and he raised his hands to his head, sinking his nails into the hairless scalp.

"Hearse-man," he said. "Tube hearse-man—bounty runner."

"He says you're dangerous," whispered the girl to Denning. "You're a tube, but you're on the run—true?"

"True."

"Catchee plain?" Carlos was addressing the entranced youth.

"Catchee straight, fright-killing—no chop."

"He says you speak the truth," said the girl. "He says the police want you because they're afraid of you. He advises"—for the first time there was a hint of amusement in her voice— "he advises Carlos, in his own interest, not to chop you."

"Feller-tube damn lucky," said Carlos with obvious regret.

The entranced youth suddenly belched, opened his eyes and shook his head dazedly. "What ride! Dopey-crazy! See

91

Earth split, see land roll like water, see sun roll across the sky—all dark—dark full of little eyes—but crazy, yes?"

At that moment the door swung open suddenly and a man entered—a man in a green suit, a hat with a high bright feather and what looked like a high-powered rifle leveled from the hip.

Before Denning had time to react, the line of teenagers turned and faced the man and, in the way that they stood was a certain menace, a reaction, an instinctive response like a cat arching its back at the sight of a dog.

It was clear that the Hunter represented something which automatically aroused the antagonism of the pulsers.

If the Hunter was aware of the atmosphere he did not show it. He had a round red face, bright dark eyes and a thin, embittered mouth.

"Stand aside, you crumbs." He swung the rifle to and fro menacingly.

No one moved; if anything, they seemed to group in front of him.

Denning realized that the pulsers were not protecting him directly—rather, it was a question of principle, of opposing an idea, a symbol of something they instinctively resented. They would protect him because, and only because, they opposed the Hunter.

The man jerked the rifle forward. "You heard me." The voice was rasping. "I'm not in this stinking hole for amusement. Stand aside, or I'll fire through you."

A girl with copper-colored eyelids and silver lashes deliberately stepped in front of the weapon. "Bang!" she said softly and challengingly.

The hunter knocked her roughly to one side with the barrel of the rifle. "Scram—gargoyle."

"Try me, tube-feller." Carlos stepped forward and took her place. His thin legs in the ballet dancer's tights looked frail and slightly bent, yet something in the way he stood was curiously menacing.

"You, too, only harder. Stand in my way and I'll slap you right into the floor."

Carlos shifted his feet slightly. "Chop, chop?" he asked softly.

The Hunter stiffened, his face losing a great deal of its aggression. Carefully, he shifted his grip on the rifle and hooked his finger round the short black trigger. "Don't you take that line of talk with me, sonny. I'm authority, I have a license to do this job. If you stand in my way, I'll blast you. I have that right; you're preventing me from carrying out my duty."

Carlos fingered the tiny weapons on his belt. "Chop, chop." This time it was a statement.

"I warned you."

Denning saw the Hunter's finger whiten as he began to squeeze the trigger and was never quite certain afterwards if he imagined what happened or if his vision had also been altered to match his other senses, but he saw in precise detail what occurred.

As the Hunter began to squeeze the trigger, Carlos, outwardly unmoved, flicked at the array of miniature weapons on the shiny belt with the index finger of his right hand.

There was a hiss and the tiny tomahawk raced away from the belt, spinning so rapidly it looked like a silver coin.

There was a click, the Hunter exhaled sighingly and something fell to the floor at his feet.

Denning stared in shocked disbelief. The Hunter was swaying, eyes bulging slightly, then he stared downward and retched. "You little bastard." He staggered and nearly fell.

That was when Denning saw that the finger which had been hooked around the trigger had been neatly severed close to the hand.

With a casualness which was as macabre as it was cold-blooded, one of the youths bent down, lifted it between

93

thumb and forefinger and offered it to him politely. "Yours, tube?"

The Hunter put his uninjured hand over his mouth and stumbled out of the room.

The girl who had translated said: "Others will come, hearse-man. There's a back way, come—"

Haltingly he tried to thank her, but she shrugged it off. "Out, tube, out—this way."

The back way was clearly an unauthorized but constructed exit which led out beneath the moving way.

"Keep walking. After about a mile, you'll find an inspection plate leading onto a catwalk between two auto factories. Get out there." Suddenly she kissed him full on the lips. "Good luck, hearse-man." The door slid shut behind him and he was alone.

Once the door was closed it was almost dark, but there were small openings at regular intervals which provided a kind of half-light.

He saw that he was in a narrow corridor which bulged at intervals with squat, plastic-encased mechanisms which, no doubt, provided power for the moving way now rolling silently some four feet above his head.

He set out in the direction the girl had indicated but had covered only a few feet when he realized that he was not alone. He nearly tripped over a man lying full length on the floor, apparently unconscious and breathing stertorously.

A few feet farther on there was another, then another and what he thought was an elderly woman muttering to herself.

It dawned upon him slowly that this was the equivalent of skid row. Here came men and women who had dreamed too many dreams, drunk too many drinks and finally reached a stage when they wanted to hide themselves from the world and from each other. People who needed but refused help, because their physical and moral decay had become a pleasure which they were loath to relinquish.

Periodically, no doubt, the authorities paid the place a visit and cleared it out, but as soon as they were gone these human derelicts would drift back.

Finally he came to the inspection plate and, after careful search, found a smooth, square surface which, at the touch of his finger, caused the plate to slide to one side.

Cautiously, he stepped out and found himself on a narrow catwalk which clung to the side of a huge squat building.

He looked right, saw the highway in the distance and stepped out briskly in the opposite direction.

The catwalk followed the line of the building and turned abruptly right as it reached the angle of the wall. He rounded it—and stopped dead.

"Going somewhere?" asked the thin-faced man in the green suit. The rifle he held pointed unwaveringly at the other's heart.

Denning sighed. "If I was, I'm not going there now, am I?"

"Too damned right you're not. I've not been walking this damned catwalk for three hours for fun—tell me, do you want to run for it, or will you take it straight like a gentleman?"

A wild hope rose in Denning that perhaps with his extra agility he might stand a chance if he ran or jumped—it was only twenty feet to the ground.

He looked quickly over his shoulder and his heart sank. A bare ten feet behind him was another Hunter.

"Mine, I think," said the new arrival.

"What the hell do you mean—yours?" The first Hunter flushed angrily. "This bird nearly impaled himself on my gun."

"Could be, but I've been tracking him for an hour."

The first Hunter scowled. "I'm not prepared to split a bounty of this size."

"Neither am I."

"You'd care to dispute this, perhaps? I must warn you, I hold the gold oak leaves of a primary duelist."

The second Hunter smiled coldly. "Awed as I am, he's still mine."

"You realize I have the drop on you, sir. My gun is already pointed."

"True, but the quarry is between us."

"Then, when the quarry moves—"

"I'm fixed," said Denning, suddenly belligerent. "I can stand here for hours."

"You can, but you won't. I propose counting to twenty. If you have not moved by then, we shall fire through you and the survivor can claim the bounty. You have twenty seconds to step aside, Quarry. One—two—"

When the count reached ten, Denning moved, but he did not step aside. He dropped flat with his legs drawn up beneath his body, ready to hurl himself forward.

There was a flash of searing white light, a gurgling scream and dull impact. Something metallic struck the ground below the catwalk.

Denning hurled himself at the nearest pair of green-clad legs.

Hunter Number Two stopped him none too gently with his foot. "A good try, old chap, quite ambitious really, but you telegraphed your intentions when you dropped. Now get up, or would you prefer me to kick in your teeth first?"

"Don't bother." Denning rose wearily and sighed. "Shall we get it over?"

"Eager?"

"There comes a time when you know you can't win. I'm sick of hanging on to life with one finger. I don't suppose you understand, but right now it seems simpler to let go."

The Hunter smiled. He had a handsome but indolently cynical face. "I understand, but I'm afraid I must disappoint you, old chap. I propose taking you in alive. Now, would you mind turning around and walking ahead? It's not only customary but safe for me, so don't get ideas. My gun is pointing straight at your back. It's not a nice weapon. Take a look at the other fellow."

Denning looked at the still body on the catwalk. The hat with its bright feather had vanished and so had half the head. What remained was cindered and unrecognizable. He jerked his eyes hastily away, feeling slightly sick.

"Right, keep walking."

Denning shrugged and obeyed. They walked for about a hundred yards and then the Hunter said "Stop. Right directly in front of you is a small green plate set in the wall. Press it with the tip of your finger."

Denning obeyed and a section of the wall slid open large enough to admit a human being.

"Don't look so startled. It's not a secret passage, only a normal inspection entrance into the auto-factory—move."

He moved and found himself on another catwalk in a vast, brightly lighted room. Level with his head and set at regular intervals round the room were groups of calibrated dials with thick red pointers.

Below, a bewildering array of machinery was in silent but constant motion.

"Auto-factory," explained the Hunter. "It makes something or other, God knows what."

"Why have you brought me here?"

The Hunter grinned twistedly. "A leading question. The average citizen doesn't know how to get into an auto-factory; consequently no one is going to search here yet." He leaned the rifle carelessly against the wall. "Call this an escape operation."

"You're on my side?"

"A little more than that—I have a personal interest. You're my biogenetic twin."

Chapter Ten

Denning stared at him. "You're joking, of course."

"Don't be trite, you've a better brain than that. Stop trying to reason this out, relax and try and *feel* something."

Wonderingly, the other tried to obey. As he did, he became slowly aware of a peculiar link between himself and the other man, and in it was a curious faculty of emotional recognition which, if not his conception of telepathy, was closely akin to it. Momentarily he found himself mentally in unison with the other but was not able to read his thoughts.

"Not yet, old chap, it just means that stage one has been carried out successfully and that now we're both on the run." He ran his fingers down the seams of the green suit which immediately parted like zips. Beneath was another suit of pastel blue. "I was never a Hunter, but I have friends. The disguise seemed a good idea at the time. By the way, the name is Liston—Mark Liston."

He sat down on the catwalk, feet dangling carelessly above the machinery, and produced a small package. "Chotein sandwiches, tastes like a chocolate spread but it's actually a concentrate. No doubt you're hungry."

"Starving." Denning realized it was true and began to wolf the sandwich ravenously.

"Take your time, they won't look here yet. In any case, I know more about this city than the original builders. As a boy I had an inquiring mind."

Denning helped himself to another sandwich. "I can never thank you properly for saving me."

"Don't overflow with gratitude, my friend. It was not

wholly noble by any means. In the first place, Veigler's enthusiasm for Project Superman was waning rapidly. When I volunteered to come to your assistance—with a certain eye to my own safety—he was unnaturally enthusiastic."

"Aren't we dependent on Veigler for our safety—don't we owe him our allegiance?"

"Brother, I'd hate to rely on Veigler now and, in answer to your second question, our allegiance is to humanity—not to individuals or parties. It's one of the things which sets us apart. As time goes on you'll see or, more aptly, feel what I mean."

"What exactly happened?"

"It's not a pretty story." Liston helped himself to the remaining sandwich and related his banishment from the zone and subsequent introduction to the Lollies. "After that, I was taken to Veigler, who made it plain from the start that I had to play ball or else. Veigler didn't want rational thinking; he wanted subservience, a brain to which he could refer on points of strategy, a super-bogeyman he could wave at the Co-temps, and an organic robot to do the dangerous dirty work. The trouble is that Veigler dreams dreams, most of which are confused, but he makes them noisy and resounding. The thinking sections of the Lolly community are not wildly enthusiastic, but the greater mass of the community are solidly behind him."

Denning brushed crumbs from his coat and lit a cigarette. "Perhaps I'd get a clearer picture if you filled in a few details. Remember, to all intents and purposes, I'm an alien here—what has Veigler in mind?"

"Sorry, I was forgetting your background." Liston lit a longer and much thinner brown cigarette of his own. "Veigler inspires his followers with the slogan 'Man versus Alien.' He speaks and dreams of his conquering armies sweeping into the Co-temp zone and slaughtering the guilty collaborators. Unfortunately, he is also a paranoic with delusions of grandeur who sees a statue erected to

99

himself in every open space and his name inscribed as savior in the pages of history. Such a man is dangerous."

Liston paused and exhaled a thin jet of smoke. "Man versus alien is an inspiring cause but, speaking to him, I soon learned that this is not his real aim. What Veigler really wants is not the destruction of the alien but a reversal of order. He wants a coordinated assault, hot and cold to defeat the Co-temps, who will then be banished to the underprivileged areas as a punishment. At which time the underprivileged will move into the temperate zone previously held by their oppressors. Having done this, he hopes to effect a deal with the aliens and, if possible, exploit their superior technology."

"But that's madness." Denning found himself unaccountably shocked. "The aliens have lost nothing; in fact, they've gained. God knows how many humans will die in that kind of attack."

"I'm glad you agree with me—see what I mean about allegiances?"

"Yes—yes, I think I do. I seem to be developing a peculiar hatred for the aliens as well. Perhaps it's the bland contempt with which they seem to be exploiting our weaknesses."

"True, that and the way you and I are made." Liston nodded grimly. "You and I were created to do a job, and it looks as if they piled on the anti-alien aspect pretty heavily. Another thing, this reversal of order business could be repeated in fifty years and again in another fifty with humanity growing weaker at each attempt. After that, of course, it might be too late."

"Too late?"

"Yes." Liston shook his head slowly. "If the planet is to support organic life of our kind, it must revolve on its axis. Oh, yes, it supports life, but let's face it—Firma is dying. In a thousand years the ice will stretch clear into the neutral zone, the shrieking winds will have died to a mild breeze because the cycles of normal convection are lessening. The winds which once raced from the cold side will crystallize and fall as ice particles. The time will come when Firma's entire atmosphere will be a snow cap, miles deep on the cold side. I don't think it will come to that, mind you; when the aliens have reduced humanity's numerical superiority to manageable proportions, they can remove the velvet glove and come down hard with the iron fist."

"What do we know about the aliens?" Denning was frowning.

"Very little. We know they are unhuman humanoids but have now successfully disguised themselves to look like men. We know they control the planet politically but have slanted both the news services and education to deny their own existence. We know also that the ship bringing them to Firma held only eighteen, but now their numbers have increased to such an extent that room must be made in the temperate zone to house them. There, apart from the fact that their normal life expectation is forty times longer than man's, confirmed information stops. I can draw a large number of conclusions from normal observation of events but, at the moment, they are of little help. Perhaps I can exploit these conclusions later, but not yet."

Denning frowned in front of him unseeingly. "Just how did you get back in the zone?"

"Ah, now, there I bow to the Lolly technicians. They've contrived a small glittering device which is left in the Z.P. patrol areas. This device, when examined closely, has the effect of breaking down the hypno-conditioning imposed on the force. The result is that a mentally enslaved man suddenly finds freedom, and all those so affected have unhesitatingly placed themselves as Lolly collaborators. Veigler hopes to free the entire force in course of time and use them as assault troops in his proposed assault."

"So you came in with a Z.P.?"

"Yes, curled up in the back of a prowl. It was damned uncomfortable." He rose. "Perhaps we'd better be moving. The heat will be concentrating on this area now."

"Where are we going?"

Liston looked at him sideways. "I hope you're not a moralist."

"Once, perhaps, not now."

"Fine, you see I have friends, all female—I make myself plain?"

"Quite plain, but it appears you lack certain vital information as regards your sex urges. Listen—"

When he had finished, Liston whistled softly. "God, if Veigler had known that he would have bounced all over the room on his head—do you realize what this means to mankind?"

"I think so—" Denning paused, frowning. "One question, there was a girl—Linda Munson. Do you know if she's—?"

Liston grinned. "Don't worry, they got her back. I never saw her, but I heard."

"Thank God."

"We'll go this way." Liston indicated the far end of the room. "Tell me your story as we go." He led the way to another inspection door and touched the plate with his finger. "Through here." He led the way through a bewildering maze of doors and passages as the other told his story.

"You've done damned well." Liston was clearly sincere. "With your sort of background it must have been hell itself."

"About the pulsers—what the hell are they?"

Liston shrugged. "The pulse emits a sub-audible rhythm, a kind of music which, apparently, is only perceived by certain adolescents. Under the stimulus of quite harmless drugs some claim forms of extrasensory perception. They are not nice groups to cross; even the police are not keen on tangling with them, but they keep to themselves and do pretty much as they like."

"And the baby weapons?"

"Energy-powered. I'm told it takes months of practice to use them effectively but, on the other hand, they are below the specifications laid down for dangerous weapons."

They emerged finally in a minor street and Liston headed directly for a building at the far end. "This is not exactly a call on a friend. At the moment, the secret police are no doubt watching my friends or, to be specific, most of my ex-mistresses." He sighed as he led the way into the building and down a corridor to the left. "It's not a pretty picture, is it? Although I understand the reasons now, I'm still not happy about it. I'm a roué from necessity rather than choice, and I suffered agonies of conscience in the early years. There was never any woman I liked enough and there was always more temptation plus a lot of invitation around the next corner. Oh, yes, I made noble resolutions at first—never again and all that sort of thing —but in the end, I had to come to terms with myself. Noble resolutions were never kept and finally I stopped making them."

He stopped at the door at the far end of the corridor and laid his finger on the announcer plate.

After a few seconds, the door slid to one side and a voice said, "Yes? What is—?" and stopped abruptly.

Denning saw an untidily dressed woman with a severely beautiful face. The blond hair was drawn so tightly back from her forehead that she looked both authoritative and cold, yet briefly there was something in the deep blue eyes which was neither cold nor authoritative.

"What do you want?" The expression was gone as quickly as it had come.

"We're coming in." Strangely, Liston had a gun in his hand. "Don't get ideas, darling; I'm not quite the same man. Further, we're both on the run—stand aside."

She obeyed silently, her body stiff and her face coldly expressionless.

Liston slid shut the door behind them and put the gun away. "This is my ex-secretary, Maria Calcott—not, as you may have gathered, one of my successes. On the other hand, I thought she liked me in a purely platonic way until the day came when I was picked up—God, she didn't bat an eyelid." He dropped into a small chair and crossed his legs, studying her almost contemptuously. "You could have been a real woman, you know, but you're afraid of yourself."

She looked at him coldly. "Have you finished? If so, I would like to go to my room and lie down. I am rather tired."

"Certainly. My friend will watch you while I disconnect the caller; you might get ideas about calling the police while you rest."

"I imagine the police will be here soon enough."

"I don't think so—no one could have failed to notice your lack of emotion." He went into the small bedroom and emerged some seconds later. "You may rest now."

"Thank you." Her voice was frigid. She left the room and slid the door shut behind her.

"That's that." Liston walked over to the auto-serve and began to punch the menu buttons. "Now we need a good solid meal before we decide about moving on."

"Can we outrun this business indefinitely?"

"Not indefinitely, but I have no intention of jumping from hideout to hideout. The truth is this: while hunting you, I had a peculiar experience. I found I had faculties which no one had told me about—a capacity for recognizing aliens. I want to repeat that experience with you there to confirm it."

A tray slid out of the delivery hatch and Liston picked it up and laid it on the table. On it was a large, well-cooked meal sufficient for two people.

"Come and eat." Liston removed knives and forks from the plastic container at the edge of the tray and laid them out for the meal. "As I was saying, if, as I suspect, we can recognize aliens, we might—" He stopped. "What are you staring at?"

Denning shrugged. "Better look behind you."

Liston turned slowly, already suspecting what had happened—it never paid to underestimate a woman, did it? Inwardly, he cursed himself for a fool. Maria Calcott stood in the open doorway, and the weapon in her hand pointed unwaveringly at his head.

"You arrogant traitor," she said, but her voice was chillingly expressionless.

He stared at her. "Traitor? Traitor to whom, for God's sake?"

Her lips tightened. "The underprivileged, the people who made your existence possible."

Liston half-rose from the table, startled. "Are you trying to tell me you're a Lolly agent?"

She did not answer the question. "I have received instructions to dispose of you or, if that was impossible, make sure you were found by the authorities."

"Good God, why?"

"You failed us. You threatened Veigler and have since tried to run things your way. That kind of behavior endangers us all, and we can't afford the risk."

Strangely, the only calm one was Denning. Casually, he picked up his knife and fork and began to eat. "Get up and take the gun away from her."

Liston scowled at him. "Why me—why not you?"

Denning swallowed a mouthful of food. "She's not in love with me," he said.

A number of conflicting emotions showed briefly in Liston's eyes, then he rose slowly from the chair and held out his hand. "Give me the gun," he said.

Her mouth tightened visibly. "You're not dealing with

105

one of your mistresses now, Liston. I've seen and heard too much of your slick charm and caressing compliments to be influenced by them now."

"Give me the gun."

"If you move another inch, I shall kill you."

He looked at her, his face expressionless. "Then you will have to kill me." He took a step towards her. "I didn't know you were an agent—how could I? I did not realize you had to play it cold and hard. I'm sorry if I hurt you."

"Stand back." Her hand shook a little.

"Give me the gun, dear, please." He took another step forward.

"You creep, you smooth-talking, treacherous creep." Her voice was a little shrill now and there were tears in her eyes. "Oh, God, it isn't fair, it's never been fair—*never*——"

Gently he took the weapon from her. "You fool," he said. "You poor damned little fool."

"Don't rub it in." Her voice was broken. "I wish I were dead."

"We'll soon alter that." He was grinning now, but inwardly experiencing a flood of unfamiliar emotion. He had never felt like this about a woman, any woman. It was as if he had waited years for the time when she would—"Come here," he said.

"You're not going to kill me?" She sounded startled.

He gripped her shoulders and drew her towards him. "Not with a gun anyway."

"Don't. Oh, God, don't, please. I'm not built to share you with a dozen others, please—"

"Why don't you shut up," he said.

Denning laid his knife and fork across the half-finished meal and picked up his plate. "This is where I finish my meal in the next room, I think." He went into the bedroom and slid the door shut behind him.

Tact, he thought, was a virtue he always appreciated in

106

others and now, surely, was the time to exercise his own. In any case, how could an experienced man like Liston—God, better not think about that now after his early blindness with Linda.

An hour later, Liston slid open the door. "You can come back now."

"Well, thanks." He picked up the empty plate and returned to the next room. "Everything settled?"

"Mark has explained everything." She smiled, and he was startled at the change in her appearance. The severe expression had gone and the fair hair, no longer drawn tightly back, fell in waves beyond her shoulders. She looked young, very feminine and almost girlish.

"You are with us?"

Momentarily her eyes clouded. "I have no choice now. Even if I didn't know Mark cared for me, I see what he's working for."

"We'll have to go." Liston was almost curt. "I can't risk endangering you now. Sooner or later, they'll search here and we must be well away before they come."

"Where will you go?"

"Don't worry, I belong to one or two exclusive clubs where the members are known only by number. It may be some time before they get around to checking them."

"But, Mark, you can't run forever."

He smiled at her gently. "We're not really running. In actual truth we're going hunting—we hope to find ourselves an alien."

"But how?" She looked alarmed.

He smiled at her gently. "We have a faculty which is not mentioned in the records—a lot of our records seem to have been unaccountably mislaid, incidentally—you see, we can *hear* them."

Chapter Eleven

They ran for three days, jumping from discreet club to lavish but secluded hotel, conscious, each time they moved, that the search was increasing in tempo. There were more Hunters in the streets, and uniformed police were making spot checks and searching buildings.

Denning noticed also that small black boxes floated about the streets in scores and occasionally swooped down over groups of people.

"Radio-controlled spy-eyes," said Liston laconically. "Someone is getting really worried. They only resort to those in extreme emergencies."

In the dining room of the fifth secluded hotel, Liston paused in the act of selecting a menu. "Do you feel something peculiar?"

Denning nodded, frowning. "Yes, I have the uncomfortable feeling that something is staring at me."

"Go on—what else?"

"Well, I can hear something, too—at least I think I can hear it— it's a sort of rustling noise coupled with a lot of minor sounds like an old-fashioned radio oscillating. What the devil is it?"

Liston grinned at him tightly. "Don't look now, don't turn around. I think we've found ourselves an alien——"

The "outward man" sitting two tables away behind Denning had a thinly handsome brown face and alert dark eyes.

His name, an unpronounceable *Srrreeth,* had, by a certain amount of phonetic juggling, been humanized to a consoling and innocuous Seathe—and Mr. Seathe was worried. It was an unfamiliar and disquieting feeling, particularly so as he was unable to account for it. One minute he had been sitting at the table, coldly complacent, and the next he found himself afflicted with unaccountable alarm.

Seathe pretended to sip his coffee, a coffee which he invariably "forgot" and left untouched because coffee was a gesture, a pretense and an act. Seathe didn't, or, more aptly, couldn't drink hot coffee. Behind the smiling, pleasant mouth with its strong, white, even teeth was no orifice to his digestive organs. In fact, behind Seathe's outward face was no face at all, only a chitinous sphere vaguely resembling a human head—a head without eyes, or mouth or any features whatever.

On the top of the head, however, cleverly concealed by the thick dark hair, yet still with room to function effectively, was a multitude of inch-long waving black antennae. With these Seathe "saw," conversed with his kind and controlled many of the scientific mechanisms of his culture.

It was a kind of sonic vision, similar to, but far more comprehensive and subtle than, that of a Terran bat.

Seathe had a black chitinous body to match his head, a body consisting of abdomen and thorax joined by a narrow, flexible, wasp-like waist. He walked upright on thin, multi-jointed legs—it had taken the aliens long practice to restrict their body movements to the limitations imposed by their native counterparts.

Seathe picked up the coffee cup and put it down again. Beneath the synthetic flesh of his hands were no hands at all, only a round black disc corresponding to the human palm, from which protruded seven wire-like tendrils.

Seathe had a black tube terminating in a cup-like nozzle hand from the center of his thorax. Through this he absorbed his food, and he breathed through orifices beneath his armpits.

He rose slowly, still trying to determine the source of his incomprehensible alarm and looked about him.

"Evening, Mr. Seathe," said a big florid man sitting at a nearby table. The florid man, like many others, thought that Seathe was human.

Seathe nodded and from force of habit Seathe "spoke" a smile. The subsonic instructions were received by the master control situated in the synthetic nose. This, in turn, activated the tiny servo-mechs concealed in the muscles of the synthetic face—the thing called Seathe smiled charmingly.

The florid man thought that Seathe was a pleasant, friendly fellow and went on with his meal.

The pleasant, friendly fellow, however, could feel his breathing orifices dilating with nervous tension. What incomprehensible thing had caused his faculties to register a danger signal?

He walked slowly from the building and hailed a taxi, but the sense of danger did not lessen; rather it seemed to follow him. Even when he paid off the taxi and entered a building, outwardly conforming with all the others but, in truth, an alien ministry, the sense of foreboding continued.

He entered the main administration room with a feeling that he was being pursued and stopped directly in front of the large human-type desk.

Krrmr (Kramer), seated behind the desk, went through the motions of looking up but he recognized instantly the sonic projections which made Seathe a familiar identity. "You are disturbed." It was a statement.

"I am, and worse, I cannot detect the cause. Perhaps I have some mental illness."

"If you suspect such an aberration," began Kramer and did not finish the sentence. "I, too!"

Their senses met and locked in an alarmed question mark. Automatically the tiny mechanisms controlling their features reproduced their inward disquiet—they "looked" at each other tensely with raised eyebrows.

"Humans come." Kramer half-rose from his chair, his senses extending beyond the door to the corridor outside. "Unusual humans. They do not conform to the sonic patterns to which we are accustomed, we——"

The door slid open and automatically he reached for the alarm plate on the surface of the desk.

Seathe, rigid with alarm, "saw" the synthetic finger extend almost to the alarm plate but never reach it. He had a hazy impression of two natives bursting into the room, a flash of searing white light and Kramer's life-emanations ceased abruptly. His blackened body slid downwards between the chair and the desk into an untidy, shapeless heap.

The leading native swung the weapon in his direction. "Unless you want to join your friend, put up your hands and don't try anything."

Seathe put them up but immediately extended his antennac to "shout" for help to others he sensed were in the next room and on the floor above.

The barrel of the weapon banged him suddenly and painfully on the side of the head. "Don't try that either. We're different—we can *hear* you." Seathe stifled the shout, hearing the air whistling through his breathing orifices in sudden and absolute terror. He spoke. A micro-device picked up his subsonic projections and translated them into the native language. "What do you want?"

"You are an alien, and the others on the floor above are also aliens. Take us to them without arousing suspicion or alarm."

"How can I do that? I am alarmed."

"Control it sufficiently to deceive them, and don't forget we can hear you."

"You will kill them all?"

"Providing you do as we say, no. We could make a deal —providing there are no tricks."

111

Seathe felt a sudden flow of assurance. A deal! There was hope then. If these humans wished to negotiate there was, in fact, more than hope. Making deals was a psychological weakness of the culture and they were poor negotiators, unskilled in subtlety and easily duped.

He bowed slightly. "This we can understand. We are a logical race, preferring reason to violence."

"Skip the opening chorus and get moving." Something prodded him roughly in the back. "Don't forget, one little trick and your friends can sweep your cinders into the nearest disposal unit—move."

He moved, assisted by a violent push from behind which almost caused him to lose his balance. The push shocked him more than the previous violence. These natives seemed abominably and frighteningly strong. Normally his race could take any one of these soft-skinned creatures apart with one hand, but these two—these two! These must be the biogenetic ones, the super-natives!

Seathe's race had no sense of humor, but they had derision. When they had first heard of these alleged super-natives, the reaction had been derisive in the extreme. These natives had entrapped themselves in their own myths and fairy stories, both of which were full of hobgoblins and impossible giants. At the moment, Seathe was inclined to the opinion that perhaps there was some basis of truth in native folklore after all.

On the next floor, the reception room was crowded but he managed to convey, in the equivalent of a human whisper, enough of the situation to have them prepared.

When they entered, *Shnun* (Shannon) had weapon drawn and pointed.

To Seathe's horror, Shannon's thorax exploded in a flash of white fire before he could fire it.

"Not quite fast enough," said one of the natives.

It was then that Seathe received a heavy blow on the

back of his head which knocked him to his knees—or the alien equivalent.

"Don't say you were not warned, friend."

Seathe made no attempt to rise, he was too dazed and horrified. As if from far away he heard the native speaking and the micro-device obligingly translated for him.

"I trust no one else wishes to shoot it out?" (Slight pause) "Take a look at this weapon. As you will observe, I press it to my hip, so, and it stays there, held firmly by the normal electromagnetic forces of the human body. We call it a reflex gun—reflexes being slightly ahead of thought, we have a time advantage. In short, the gun leaps to the hand and not the hand to the gun. These weapons have been directly tuned to our individual nervous systems. As you have seen, we can draw, aim and fire faster than any of you, with a gun already pointed, can squeeze a trigger." (Fractional pause). "Would any of you alien gentlemen care for another demonstration?"

Seathe heard no reply, but he felt the surge of consternation and fear which told him, at least, that the demonstration of force had been clearly understood. No one was going to risk shooting it out with these natives.

It struck him suddenly as incongruous that this race— irrespective of these two biogenetics—so pathetically soft-fleshed and puny should be so steeped in violence. Always they fought in terms of force and direct aggression, whereas his own culture, physically ten times stronger, preferred manipulation and subtlety to achieve their aims.

There was a movement among those facing him, and with relief Seathe saw *Grndn* (Grandon) the Director of Expansion (Diplomatic Branch) step forward.

"Gentlemen, there is no need for violence." Outwardly Grandon was a charming middle-aged man with a distinguished touch of gray at the temples. "Please, sit down, gentlemen—chairs for our guests, please, Mr. Hardy." He smiled. "Don't be alarmed; there will be no treachery."

113

The taller of the two natives spun his weapon deftly around his finger. "Very few of you will live to profit by it if there is."

"I may rise now?" inquired Seathe.

"You may, and if you have a God, thank him. You're very damned lucky to be alive."

Seathe said, "Yes," meekly, realizing it was true.

The natives sat down slowly after first examining the chairs carefully.

The tall one waved his gun. "Before we get down to business, get that body out of the way. I find it repulsive." He smiled unpleasantly and added, "Even if it is dead."

He waited while the body was removed. Someone brought a chair for Grandon and he sat down facing them.

He smiled. "Let me see now—Liston and Denning, isn't it? We have heard much of you but I must confess we were not prepared for a two-man invasion. Tell me, gentlemen, what do you hope to gain?"

"As you may have guessed, we have a sort of mission. At the moment you are hostages."

"Mission? Surely vendetta would be a better word, Mr. Liston?"

"Does it matter? If by vendetta I can achieve my ends, the word 'mission' is still applicable."

Grandon "spoke" a smile. For a servo-mech grimace it was a brilliant exposition of subtlety. It was chiding, sad and faintly deprecating. "My dear Mr. Liston, much as I admire your ambition and determination, your chance of success is, to say the least, infinitesimal." He spread his pink convincing hands in a wholly human gesture. "Now, why not be reasonable? We bear you no ill-will. You may leave without interference and there will be no reprisals."

"Really? I have no doubt that half the secret police are now surrounding the building all ready to shoot us down as soon as we appear."

"We can arrange for safe conduct."

114

Liston showed his teeth but did not reply.

"We can broadcast direct orders."

The other laughed. "My God, you slay me—or am I being prophetic? Do you think we are quite without intelligence?"

"On the contrary, we are appealing to your intelligence for, you see, you stand no chance, no chance whatever. Oh, yes, you hold a few of us at gun point but, as you are probably aware, there are many others. Again, and I will concede the point, this is a brilliant maneuver except for one small fact—support to back it up."

He leaned forward slightly, the synthetic features benevolent and almost concerned. "I hate to put this so brutally, my friends, but when you first arrived in the zone you had the backing of a subversive organization. You had allies, you had friends, but now you have none. Every man's hand is turned against you. In short—Veigler has sold you out."

Liston crossed his legs comfortably and grinned. "How many pieces of silver?"

"You don't believe us? Very well, if you have no objection to seeing the recorded interview we will prove it to you. I must apologize in advance however for the poor quality of the reproduction. Mr. Veigler bounced his message off so many substations in order to conceal his exact whereabouts that the picture suffers accordingly—will you see the recording?"

Liston nodded. "Certainly, but run off a few copies. I'd like to study them later."

Grandon bowed. "As many as you wish, Mr. Liston. In fact, I feel there is much in this recording from which all could profit. Our position on this planet is so often misunderstood and misrepresented that this recording should do much to clear the air. It is abundantly clear that you, too, share the misapprehensions of many of your race. You see, we are not invaders. However, I will let the recording do the explaining."

115

Denning, outwardly taking a passive part in the operation, watched the opposite wall apparently disappear and the image of Grandon slowly appear. Almost immediately, another image appeared opposite him, the image of a myopic little man seated in a chair, a man he concluded correctly must be Veigler.

Denning was not quite so passive as he appeared. Although still a little dazed and incredulous at the position in which he found himself, he was still doing a job—he was listening intently. He was listening to the subaudible rustlings, flutings and oscillations of the alien language and learning it rapidly. He could never hope to reproduce it in conversation, but in a very short time he would *understand* it completely. Grandon, intent on talking his way out of a dangerous situation, was unwittingly providing the perfect lesson.

There would be the rustling sounds of the alien language, a fractional pause for the translator to complete its task, then out would come the rustling sounds in human tongue. Already Denning had a working basis, and in another hour or so and no alien would be able to speak without his understanding.

Basically it was a simple language, one word sufficing in the place of many human ones. For example, the words "we understand" consisted only of the single word "understand," the "we," "I" or "you" being determined by the slight shortening or lengthening of the same word. The tense was changed by the slightest inflection from "understand" to "understood."

Mentally, despite its alien origin, Denning took off his hat to the translating device. It took one fluting sound, one squeak and a rustle and got two complete human sentences out of it.

Opposite him the two images solidified and became three dimensional. The recording had begun.

Veigler opened the play. "If you have any hopes of

tracing this call, think again." The little eyes were bright, moist and nervous. "You know who I am, I take it?"

"We know. What is the purpose of your call?"

"A deal. I am given to understand you like deals, providing you come out of them with an overall advantage."

"Have you called us for a slanging match or have you some concrete and rational proposal?"

Veigler blinked, clearly unprepared for this sort of reaction. "I have certain information which might be of value. I also have a proposal which might be of use to you."

"Let us hear the proposal first."

"The humans in the zone—your zone—have enjoyed the benefits of collaboration long enough. It's about time they got out to make room for the more vital sections of society —ours."

"And that is your proposition, Mr. Veigler?"

"It is, with or without your cooperation. You see, I am now strong enough to come in and kick them out and, even if I failed, you'd be a primary target in an all-out attack and a lot of you might get knocked off."

"And the alternative?"

"Consider the proposal. Cooperate and you stay on, providing of course, you continue to cooperate."

Grandon bowed a little mockingly. "Hardly a subtle approach—if we cooperate, you will move in and exploit us. If we do not cooperate, you will attack with the intention of destroying us—correct?"

Veigler nodded triumphantly. "Exactly."

Chapter Twelve

Grandon appeared to consider the matter, then he said, "And your information?"

"Without going into details, you have two biogenetic human males in your zone. They are far more dangerous to your kind than you may imagine."

"If they are so dangerous, why do you tell us?"

Veigler leaned back slightly, obviously gaining confidence. "I'll be frank with you. We suspect that they may be equally dangerous to us. As part of our bargain I would be prepared to pass on all available records."

Grandon's image stroked its chin thoughtfully, then appeared to reach a decision. "Mr. Veigler, before we go into the question of your information and decide its value, perhaps it would help if you told us why you organize violence against us."

"What!" Veigler looked completely taken aback. "My God, you've got a nerve asking me *that*."

"Have we, Mr. Veigler?" Grandon's synthetic voice was soft but compelling. "Has it ever occurred to you that we don't know what you've been told? Have you ever paused to consider that you are equally the victim of several generations of misleading propaganda?"

"Do you think I'm a fool!" Veigler's face was flushed and angry.

"On the contrary, we regard you as a man of intelligence." Grandon paused, meaningfully. "Which is why we might consider your proposition as a reasonable proposal, couched that is in less aggressive terms."

"You'd consider it?" Veigler's face was dark with suspicion.

"Most certainly—we're rather tired of being scapegoats. Every indignity, every cruelty which occurs in the under-privileged areas is laid at our door. Nothing is said of the cruelty man inflicts on man, yet, Mr. Veigler, it is clear that you suspect, that you have insight, or you would not hate the inhabitants of this zone with such intensity."

Veigler's face twitched. Clearly he was torn with con-flicting emotions, and equally clearly the subtle flattery of Grandon was finding weak spots and exploiting his ego-tism.

The alien was quick to force his advantage home. "Oh, yes, we know what you think, and to lesser intelligences an explanation would be a waste of time—may I lead you through this step by step?" He did not wait for an answer. "Mr. Veigler, I am sure you have consulted the records. Tell me, how many of my people came to Firma and in how many ships?"

Veigler scowled at him, shifting uncomfortably in the chair. "According to the records, there was one ship con-taining eighteen aliens."

Grandon smiled gently. "Mr. Veigler, as a man of in-telligence, do you honestly consider that one ship and eighteen men constitutes an invasion force?"

"Damn you, you managed to conquer the world all the same."

"Did we? Is there anything in the records to prove it? Can you quote a single instance in which we have offered violence to any of your kind?"

"It's all very well to talk, but facts speak for themselves."

"Facts speak according to the order in which they are arranged. May I suggest you listen first and decide after-wards."

"Very well." It was clear that Veigler was completely out of his depth and needed time to think.

Grandon didn't give him any. "Contrary to propaganda and general opinion, we came to your planet not as invaders but as refugees. Just as—and you may consult your own history—many of your people ran to new lands for refuge. Our plight was desperate. We had traveled countless light years; many of us were sick; supplies were low, our vessel urgently in need of overhaul and repair. We went into orbit around this planet, tapped your communication channels and learned your language. Then we broadcast an appeal to your entire people for help, for at least a temporary haven where we could repair our vessel and attend to our sick."

Grandon paused, then continued. "Shall I tell you what happened then, Mr. Veigler, or can you guess? Your world divided against itself, some for and some against, a widening division which led to riots and finally civil war. In this war those for us, the compassionate and humane sections of your race, finally achieved ascendancy and we were permitted to land. We had been here a bare few days, however, when those who had been opposed to us launched a counterattack of such violence that those who had befriended us were flung back on almost every sector with grievous losses. It was clear that within a month they would be utterly defeated. They appealed to us for help."

The image of Grandon leaned towards the image of Veigler. "What would you have done in our case, my friend? Would you have abandoned those who had risked and sacrificed so much to aid you? Tell me what you would have done?"

Veigler blinked at him moistly and uneasily. "Well, it's a little difficult——"

"It was difficult for us, too, Mr. Veigler, but we did what we feel sure you would have done. We stood by our friends. It was not an easy decision. There were only eighteen of us and our entire armory consisted only of four hand weapons of limited range. Our race is, however, highly skilled in the science of what we are pleased to call 'special dynamics,' which pertains particularly to the orbit and rotation of planetary bodies. Consequently, and in desperation, we jury-rigged a device which slowed and finally stopped the rotation of your planet on its axis. Needless to say, the repercussions completely stalled the triumphant attack. In the subsequent earthquakes, hurricanes, cloudbursts and tidal disturbances, the attacks withered away."

Grandon sighed. "We thought that within a year or so enmity would die and old hatreds be forgotten; instead, they increased. We were compelled to maintain conditions to prevent a planet-wide war that would have destroyed everyone."

Grandon paused again, just long enough to let the picture sink in. "Mr. Veigler, *we* did not want a divided race; *we* did not want underprivileged areas. They were maintained by men; hatred was fanned by men. Our position in your society is wholly neutral. As far as we are concerned, you or any of your people could walk into this zone today and we would not lift a finger to stop you. On the other hand, the descendants of our benefactors, now alas sunk into moral decay, would still from fear and hatred try to destroy you. Do I make my point, sir? Your real enemies are the members of your own race."

Veigler licked his lips. What he had heard fitted in neatly with his own plans, and he was half-convinced.

Grandon pushed his advantage home. "We do not, as you may believe, control the government and the police, but we have one great advantage, one great lever which we have never used—our control of this planet's rotation. We are prepared to exercise this advantage now in your favor, to abandon our neutrality for a few days for the furtherance of peace. We have said you may come into this zone, that you are as welcome here as the descendants of our benefactors. Now we will prove this. We will send a fleet of ground cars for you and any of your government you care to bring. We will personally guarantee your safe arrival and your safe return."

The image of Veigler looked at the image of Grandon sideways, furtively and twisted with suspicion. "What sort of bloody fool do you take me for? That I should walk into a trap like that—hell!"

"You jump to conclusions, Mr. Veigler. You did not wait for the rest of our proposition. Would you regard it as a trap if four of our race first presented themselves in your zone as a guarantee of your safety?"

Veigler's mouth twitched, his hands clenched and his forehead puckered with thought. Clearly he suspected a trap, but it was equally clear he was unable to see one.

'Short of actual surgery you may examine our deputation on arrival. For instance, instead of synthetic flesh concealing their hands, the deputation will wear special gloves —will that satisfy you?"

Veigler exhaled hissingly. If unconvinced, he was obviously impressed. "It seems fair enough. What have you in mind? You made a proposition for certain ends, what ends?"

"No, Mr. Veigler, you made the proposition, remember? Agreement could be better reached in circumstances of mutual trust. Shall we get down to the arrangements for your visit?"

There was a hissing sound and the picture blurred, wavered and vanished abruptly.

Grandon looked directly at Liston and Denning. "You saw, you heard and much was explained. Perhaps you, too, were laboring under a misapprehension; perhaps you, too, are victims of your own propaganda."

Liston smiled coldly. "And perhaps not, but for a con-line I raise my hat to you."

"Con-line?"

Liston smiled again. "Con-line might be described as the confidence trickster's sales talk. That's what you are, alien con-men, sweet-talking your way into the acquisition of an empire."

Briefly Grandon's features twitched as if he had temporarily lost control of the synthetic muscles, and then he was his normal suave self again. "We strike you as so insincere?"

"Insincere! Your story is so full of holes that I don't have to push it aside to see the light. I won't go into it in detail, but I find it singularly unlikely that by a stroke of good fortune you just *happened* to have the necessary equipment to brake the axial rotation of a planet. Shall I tell you the true story? You landed in secret, 'cased' the psychology of the inhabitants and then went to work on those you could exploit. You backed the malcontents, the ruthlessly ambitious, the idiot-men who saw themselves as God-given leaders. You backed these puppets with every device in your superior technology until they achieved positions of power. Finally, however, authority woke up to your existence, but you were prepared for that. You had an unpleasant device which stopped the planet in its tracks and, at the same time, neatly cut the race of man into three manageable portions. This, needless to say, stopped real opposition before it had properly begun."

Liston paused and spun the gun meaningfully. "Do you still have the damned insolence to sit there and ask me if I think you're insincere?"

Grandon shrugged faintly. "The dividing line between misapprehension and fixation is narrower than I imagined."

"Nicely put. Now I'll have copies of that recording please."

"As you wish. Will ten be sufficient? Fetch them, please, Maynard."

Maynard turned as if to obey, but Denning was there before him. "One moment." He swung a cupped open hand savagely. There was a brittle crumpling sound and Maynard toppled sideways and lay still, his synthetic features curiously lopsided.

123

"He had ideas," Denning explained. "He was going to include an anti-personnel grenade in the handful of recordings. I heard him discussing it in the equivalent of undertones before he left."

"You *understand* us?" Grandon's features appeared afflicted with curious spasms.

"I do now, thanks to you." Denning made a gesture at the body on the floor. "Get rid of it."

"He's only stunned, surely——"

"He's dead. I wasn't playing." Denning heard the flood of consternation and smiled grimly. This was the final lesson.

"The recordings." Liston extended his hand.

Shakily, and in obvious terror, they handed the recordings to him.

"Not so good without the devices of treachery, are you?" He pocketed the recordings and smiled coldly.

Grandon, his face twitching, said, "You cannot win." He sounded desperate. "You are alone, friendless. In the long run, it will be our victory."

"On the contrary, in the long run it will be ours. In hours, or if we are lucky, days, you will find a way of outwitting us, but you are only postponing the inevitable. You cannot win. Listen."

When he had finished, Grandon seemed temporarily to have lost control of his features, the synthetic flesh writhing and twitching unpleasantly.

Liston waited until he had regained control, then flipped his gun in the air and caught it deftly. "Let us deal with the present. Right now you are hostages. Denning has heard enough to know you are key experts so if anything happens to you, your project folds up and, incidentally, your possible escape. Four of you are needed to get your ship off this planet—right? Remember, my alien friends, we are giving you an alternative—withdrawal. Our successors may be less kindly disposed."

124

He laughed softly. "However, now you will do as we say." He jerked the gun at Grandon. "You will call the Ministry of Security and you will instruct Kostain to obey orders with your life as forfeit, understood? You will tell him that a number of calls will be made from this building and, under no circumstances, are the calls to be tapped or the recipients watched, arrested, threatened or in any way molested. Tell him that if he disobeys I will give you permission to contact those members of your race outside this building and they will deal with him personally—clear?"

"Quite clear." The translator managed to convey extreme bitterness, and Grandon walked stiffly to the recorder.

Liston stood there with the gun in his back while he made the call.

"Fine, now go and sit down—watch them, Denning." He switched on the privacy unit which successfully cut off his voice from those in the room and dialed a number. "Hello, darling, Mark here. This has to be brief because I haven't much time. Have you a friendly oppo, a special one who might take a special kind of message and deliver it in the right quarters?—You have, good. Listen, I am sending you a special message and some recordings. I want both the message and the recordings to reach the intellectuals, the scientists and the technical experts in the community—You can do that, good. Oh, yes, and another thing, I may send you a message that Veigler has been killed. The message may not be true but pass it on anyway——"

A minute or so later he nodded to Denning. "Your turn now. As we agreed, it's worth a try. I've written down both numbers on the pad."

Denning went over and dialed. Within a few seconds a face appeared.

"Well, well, dear boy, how nice. What can I do for you?"

125

Denning grinned at him a little stiffly. "You owe me a favor, Marko——"

Three minutes later Marko's face had been replaced by another. "What, Hearse-man?"

Denning knew he had to be quick. "Listen, Carlos, I'm not asking any favors, only that you hear what I have to say. After that you can forget it or get someone to ride it, okay?"

Carlos blinked at him bitterly. "Catchee." He listened. When Denning had finished, he shrugged. "Tube-stuff. To me you're gut-hate, Hearse-man. Maybe I'll auction it around for a dream, maybe not." He vanished slowly as contact was broken at the other end.

He nodded to Liston. "Perhaps, perhaps not."

Liston shrugged. "Right, now for the main call of the day. I've been aching for this one, haven't spoken to my friend Kostain since he sent me out to freeze to death." He went over to the caller, switched on the privacy unit and dialed a number. . . .

In the Ministry of Security, Kostain touched the contact plate and a face appeared, a handsome, indolent face which was all too familiar.

"Well, well, we meet again!"

Kostain's mouth tightened, but he said evenly, "Are you mad, Liston? Do you think you can hold these people as hostages indefinitely?"

"Not indefinitely, but long enough."

"Don't boast, my friend. We have the building completely surrounded. We can come in and take it any time."

"When you start coming in, Kostain, aliens start dying. They know that and so do you. That's why your men are still outside."

"Is that why you called me—to boast?"

"No, I called to give you a friendly warning."

"How charming. You hope to hold me to ransom, perhaps?"

Liston laughed softly. "You speak as if you own the world, Kostain, but you only run it the way you're told. You don't hold the whip."

"Ah! A lecture. I might have known."

"Oh, no. I see you're at the top of the tree, but you're stuck there and the branches at the top are damned thin. One tiny mistake, one wrong movement and you're out, Kostain, out and falling." He paused, his face thoughtful. "I'm sending you a recording, complete with an official stamp to prove its authenticity. Take a look at it and wonder. Is Grandon laying an elaborate trap for Veigler, or is this a scheme to double-cross you and, at the same time, reduce humanity's numerical superiority even more?"

He paused and lit a cigarette. "Veigler arrives tomorrow, doesn't he?"

"Yes." Kostain looked puzzled.

"Suppose something happens to him?"

"It won't. We have the strictest instructions."

"Care to bet?"

"What the hell are you driving at, Liston?" For the first time Kostain looked worried.

"As a starter, if something does happen, guess who will take the blame? Secondly, my guess is that Veigler won't be among those present, but a man very much like him. When the double gets rubbed out, Veigler will scream treachery and strike. It's exactly the kind of excuse he's been waiting for. I don't think for a moment he can win, but I think he's strong enough to fight his way into the suburbs and cause a hell of a lot a damage. You can guess who will be held responsible for that, too. On the other hand, if he's reached agreement with the aliens, perhaps he'll win, not that I think they're stupid enough to let him. My guess is they'll secretly back both sides, allowing them to destroy each other in thousands——"

Chapter Thirteen

Kostain shifted uneasily, conscious of a fluttering coldness in the pit of his stomach. There was something about Liston's story which had a ring of truth.

"Kostain."

"Yes."

"You still have a choice, you know. Man or alien, don't waste too much time deciding which; there is no middle road." There was a faint click and the image blurred and slowly vanished.

Six minutes later, the recordings arrived by transmitter service.

Kostain played it back twice, feeling the coldness in his stomach increase.

"Tovin, I don't like this."

"No, sir." Tovin's face was a doughy, neutral blank, his voice expressionless.

"Nothing must happen to Veigler."

"Oh, no, sir, no—I will treble the guards, check every roof and building. I will attend to it now."

"Good." Kostain's thin, beautiful face was so colorless that it looked almost saintly. "Oh, and Tovin——"

"Sir?" Tovin, about to leave, halted.

"I have a thought." Kostain smiled bitterly. "I have a thought that you were going to make a call, a discreet call to certain of the Masters. You were going to tell them, were you not, that I have become a security risk?"

"I, sir? The thought never——"

"Spare me the protestations, Tovin." He leaned back in his chair and shook his head slowly. "Shall I tell you something, my friend? I am going to let you. After you have heard me. Sit down, Tovin."

"Yes, sir." Tovin sat, perplexed and alarmed.

Kostain lit a cigarette and let the smoke trickle through his nostrils. "You are a simple man, Tovin, a man of inspired cunning but without subtlety. You see yourself stepping into my shoes with the blessing of the Masters, but it is not, alas, quite so simple. Assume for one moment that what Liston says is true. Suppose Veigler sends a double and the double is assassinated. Suppose further that you see the assassination begin. You see someone in the watching crowds draw a gun and point it—what would you do?"

"I would shoot him down as ordered, sir."

"Would you, Tovin, would you? And suppose, just for one moment, that the would-be assassin wears the distinguishing marks of a Master?"

"Oh, my God!" Tovin's face was suddenly colorless. He was seeing the situation with horrible clarity. To the crowd the assassin would be just another man, but to any member of the secret police certain peculiarities of clothing would instantly distinguish him as a Master.

Kostain rose slowly. "It's a nice desk, try it for size. Of course, the problem I have just mentioned goes with it—but it's all yours." He smiled, showing his perfect teeth. "Make your call, Tovin, here or outside."

Tovin did not move, his hands were clenched and a bead of sweat crawled down his left temple. "What do we do, sir?" It was clear that Tovin had given up all thoughts of betrayal and was unashamedly terrified.

"Ah, that's better. I hope it is now clear that if we fall, we fall together."

"Truly, sir, I——"

"Save it, save it. As to what we do, we can only decide that when the time comes."

"But that's tomorrow, sir, only a few hours——"

"I know. Get your men among those crowds early. I want a direct report on the first Master seen among them."

"Yes, sir." Tovin went.

Sixteen hours later, his image built up in the receptor unit. "There's a Master at intersection thirty-four, sir."

"That's about half-way along the route isn't it?"

"Yes, sir. Veigler's convoy is due in about thirty-five minutes."

"I see." Kostain looked pale and nervous. There were smudges beneath his eyes, and the skin looked as if it had been sewn at the corners of the mouth and drawn tight over the cheekbones. He drummed his fingers irritably on the desk and scowled unseeingly in front of him.

In truth he had not closed his eyes for nearly forty hours and had spent the last sixteen pacing the floor of his office.

Finally he said, "I want six men directly behind him, plain clothes agents—understood?"

"Yes, sir"— Tovin hesitated, swallowed and was visibly sweating— "Sir, we checked him with a frisk-ray. He's armed, sir; he's packing one of their blast-sticks in his right sleeve. What shall I do?"

Kostain felt sweat dampen his own face. He'd hoped, willed, almost prayed, that this situation would never arise, but now it had; now he was faced with it and, worse, he had to do something about it.

His mouth thinned suddenly and he leaned forward, both hands flat on the surface of his desk. "If he tries to use it—" He swallowed, trying to steady his voice. "If he tries to use it, gun the bastard down."

In his secret headquarters beneath the ice, Veigler paced restlessly up and down. Occasionally his lips twisted, periodically he nibbled the nail of his right thumb, and his eyes were darting, furtive and bright with cunning.

They thought he was a fool! They said, "Walk into my parlor" and they thought he'd walk, but he was far too clever for that. Oh, yes, Standel had gone, dedicated and

130

full of fervor. "Yes, Leader. No, Leader" and "I can handle it, trust me." Trust him! Standel was a groveling idiot with a death wish, a compulsive martyr who, fortunately, bore a strong physical resemblance to himself. A few deft touches with a flesh pencil, some minor surgery to tighten the skin and Standel had become Veigler's double.

So Standel had gone in the ground car. Standel, upheld by his dedication to a leader-figure, had taken the place of the fly and obligingly walked into the parlor.

Of course, if Standel survived, a "switch" might be undertaken later, but Veigler was quite certain that Standel wouldn't survive. Somewhere there was treachery, although it was difficult to tell where, but after a time you developed a sixth sense—*you knew*.

It was true that the aliens had sent their deputation of four as a guarantee of good faith but even so——

A guard appeared and saluted. "Science-adviser Dalkeith, sir."

"Send him in." Veigler sat down at his desk, almost glad of a diversion.

Dalkeith came in unhurriedly. He was a tall, dark-skinned man with untidy brown hair and a thin, sardonic mouth.

"Robots." He dropped into the only available chair and began to roll himself a cigarette from some black synthetic tobacco.

Veigler half-rose, too startled to reprimand the other for his lack of respect. "What did you say?"

"I said robots." Dalkeith lit his cigarette. "Damn good ones with a neat chitinous covering, but still robots."

"You are quite sure?"

"I've a Stirling-Gasson right under their feet. Unless your visitors have reactive hearts with a 1.09 nuclear output and a fluctuating circuit, your friends are robots."

Veigler resumed his seat slowly, two patches of color high on each cheek. Then he banged his fist down on the

desk. "Treachery! I knew it was treachery, I felt it here."
He pressed his hand to his heart. "I have insight, you
know, a sixth sense, a guardian spirit——"

"Make up your damned mind," said Dalkeith, tiredly.

Fortunately, Veigler didn't hear him. He was working
himself into one of his furies. "They won't get away with
this! Guarantee of good faith indeed! I expected something like this, *expected* it! You know what this means,
don't you, Dalkeith? This means action, this means mobili-
zation and attack. I shall give orders to that effect now."

Dalkeith smiled sadly and shook his head. "How can
you? You've been dead six hours."

Veigler stared at him, aware for the first time of a
distinct change in Dalkeith's normal tones.

Dalkeith exhaled smoke. "According to a certain report,
your ground car was blasted to pieces by someone in the
watching crowds—sad, isn't it? I see you're breaking your
heart over Standel."

Veigler half-rose. "Guards! *Guards!*"

"Perhaps they can hear you." Dalkeith crossed his legs.
"But I doubt very much if they can do anything about it,
not with a gun pressed against their bellies."

"This is mutiny." Veigler sounded short of breath.

"Correct, but it's not quite such a nasty word as treachery, is it? Some hours ago, I and several others received a
most interesting recording of you making a deal with your
sworn enemies. We found it startlingly different from your
public announcement of an ultimatum. In view of these
facts, certain of us decided to take over before you sacrificed half the race on the altar of your intolerable conceit."

Veigler's eyes protruded slightly. "You swore allegiance;
you promised to follow——"

"Shall we be frank? In those days there wasn't much
else to follow and the opposition had a rough time. Further,
your slogan was 'Man versus Alien' and we believed you.

132

We no longer believe you. Your real slogan is man versus man."

Veigler experienced a rare flash of insight. "Liston and Denning are responsible for this."

"They sent us recordings of your little deal, yes. They also pointed out the dangers of your kind of attack; they left the rest to us."

"You are easily deceived, Dalkeith. These men are genetic monsters, unbalanced neurotics, posturing adventurers without sense of rightness or responsibility."

"It seems to me your posturing adventurers have achieved more in six weeks than you achieved in ten years."

"Some instruments make a louder noise than others."

"*You* say that." Dalkeith laughed insultingly. "God, how many harangues have you inflicted on us in the last ten years! No, the truth is, Veigler, you hoped the supermen would be a complement to your own ego. You wanted to wield them as extensions of your own ideas and personality. When, however, they proved themselves individuals with alert, logical minds and with views of their own, you became alarmed. You saw your star waning, the thunder snatched from your glory, and you sold them out to the aliens regardless of what your treachery might do to the race of man."

"When these creatures have tried and failed you will think differently. They cannot hold these aliens to ransom indefinitely."

"They realize that, but they had an idea for altering the situation which they referred to us. Fortunately, we were equipped to meet their request and their suggestion has not only been perfected but is in full scale production. . . ."

In the Co-temp zone, the aliens were becoming a little desperate. Grandon had long since abandoned all hope of catching the two natives off-guard. They slept in turns, apparently quite content to sit it out indefinitely. The position was further complicated by the fact that discussion and plan were ruled out by the knowledge that the natives could hear and understand every word that was said.

The caller went on, and Liston touched the reception plate.

"It's for you." There was something in his expression which a human would have called mocking but to an alien was directly contemptuous.

Warily, suspecting some sort of trick, Grandon took the call. A three-dimensional image had, however, already built up in the instrument.

Grandon recognized the caller. It was *Vlf* (Ralph), Director of Biology, and Ralph's synthetic features were clearly beyond the control of the servo-mechs. "Turner has been killed; our own forces have turned against us. He was shot to pieces by the native police. The ground cars from the cold areas have entered the zone unharmed."

Grandon said nothing, drearily aware that there was nothing to say. In normal circumstances, the situation was not irretrievable but now—Abruptly he broke contact, aware that the whole project was collapsing about him.

Liston smiled at him without triumph. "You had to learn, Grandon, you had to learn that when it comes to a real decision, man will back man."

"What do you want?" The alien had suddenly lost faith in himself and the whole project.

"We told you once, but you stalled for time. Restore the axial rotation of the planet and leave while you have a chance."

Grandon sat down, no longer bothering to conceal the multi-jointed pliability of his body. "You oversimplify, Liston; axial rotation cannot be started without appalling physical repercussions." He made a fluid and curiously expressive gesture with his hand. "Flood, tempest, eruption, one upon another. People will die, and in the fury of the survivors we shall be sacrificed. Believe us or not, it is the truth."

"We believe you, we expected it. We propose moving all the women and children into this zone for safety."

"And the rest?"

"Into the neutral zones."

"You are a dreamer, Liston. They will perish within a week."

"Then it's up to you to devise and erect adequate safety shelters, isn't it? They'd better be damned good ones, because you're coming out there with us, carefully dispersed just in case some of those shelters fail to come up to standard."

"The others outside this building will never agree."

"They will because you are going to call them in, a few at a time, whereupon they will be persuaded."

"You cannot hold us all as hostages. Try holding nearly two hundred of us at gun point."

"Strange as it may seem, we think we can. Special equipment is on its way here now."

Dalkeith arrived six hours later, accompanied by his scientific team and ten ground cars laden with equipment. He had a strong escort of police and entered the zone without incident, but he sensed, despite changes, there was still no love lost. The faces of the police were cold and resentful and they avoided looking at him directly. They were obeying orders, but they would have shot him out of hand as a Lolly insurgent at the drop of a hat.

He had only time to glance wonderingly at the sun, and then he was hustled into a huge squat building which resembled a small pyramidal mountain.

Unfamiliar robotic devices removed his equipment from the ground cars and brought it in behind him.

After emerging from an elevator he was conducted into a large but crowded room.

"You got them?"

"Yes, with a dozen or so spares."

"Was it difficult?"

"Not difficult to devise but a hell of a race against time to produce the required number. It's a hell of an idea. I wish I'd thought of it."

Liston laughed softly. "Don't belittle yourself. I only *thought* of it. It took an expert like you to make something from a wild idea." He held out his hand. "We've met before in a verbal kind of way, I believe. Unless I'm mistaken, you talked me in when I was thrown out of the zone. God, how I hated your sneering voice, but it needled me into adapting—I owe you my life."

Dalkeith shook the proffered hand and stared at him wonderingly. "You still recognize my voice after hearing me over a lousy beam like that?"

Liston smiled a little tiredly. "I have rather unusual hearing, one of my biogenetic assets."

A robotic device rolled through the doorway with a huge crate which it placed on the floor.

"Are these the ornaments?"

"All ready for distribution." Dalkeith smiled, suddenly confident. "When do we start making presentations?"

"Right now—you there, come here."

Grandon obeyed, feeling a strange inexplicable terror. What had these natives in store for him now?

"Bend forward."

He obeyed and felt something snapped at the back of his neck.

"Right, next."

Grandon straightened and saw that a metal chain had been fastened around his neck. Hung on the chain was a small bright pendant.

The other native, Denning, usually so quiet, smiled at

him. "You asked us once how long we thought we could hold you at gun point, we can give you an answer now—indefinitely. The pendant on that chain holds two fissionable elements which, if brought together, become critical. Fortunately for you, however, a transmitter—concealed elsewhere—is continually broadcasting a power impulse to hold those elements apart. As you will have observed, the chain can only be removed by breaking the links and, if you do that, you break the circuit. If you break the circuit, the two elements come together—you follow me, I hope?" He did not wait for Grandon to answer. "All the while you obey orders our transmitter will remain in operation; if you attempt revolt or treachery, we shall simply turn it off."

Grandon's synthetic features could not pale, but he experienced an alien equivalent—his breathing orifices contracted to agonizing smallness and for a moment he swayed on his feet. It was not the immediate danger which affected him so much as the diabolical ingenuity of the scheme. With a live executioner already at his throat, his race had no option but to obey.

Bitter thoughts chased through his mind. If he ever escaped to his own sector of the galaxy, his primary report would deplete the personnel of every scientific institute in the empire. At least thirty experts from Alien Psychology would undoubtedly end up in slow-incinerator cubicles and as for Survey. . . . The ingenuity factor of this race had been grossly underestimated, and the fact that the whole project had been brought to disaster by a device from a *technically inferior* culture would bring government executions as well.

Chapter Fourteen

Liston's voice jerked him out of his reverie.

"Grandon, you can bring in the others now. I want them in batches of ten. You'd better explain the situation to them as they come in."

Grandon said, "Yes—yes, I will do that." The translator caught and expressed the listlessness of his feelings perfectly.

When it was over, when all his race were decorated with a chain and pendant, he walked tiredly to the window and stared down into the street at the men and women below. Weak, soft-fleshed worms, travesties of advanced intelligences, but they'd beaten him. His thoughts began to wander but he lacked the energy to discipline them. Yes, soft-fleshed, belligerent and generally stupid, but containing some spark which the surveyors had missed. Perhaps it was understandable; biologically these creatures were almost amoeba, still needing two sexes to procreate their kind. His own race had advanced beyond this stage to a mal-neuter culture which, at given periods, became bisexual wherein each individual was capable of fertilizing and laying several soft-skinned eggs for the continuance of the race. It had always struck him as——

From below came a sharp if slightly muffled explosion. Grandon looked, saw a flash and puff of white smoke. When the smoke drifted away, there was a blackened and headless body lying just beyond the wide steps leading up to the building.

"One of your race didn't believe you," said Liston, softly. "One of them thought we were bluffing and broke his chain. I don't think anyone else will try it, do you?"

Grandon did not answer. He was suddenly weary to the point of collapse. He leaned tiredly against the wall. "You are enjoying your triumph, yes? You are a sadist, Liston."

"Both accusations are perhaps true, but I *care,* I *feel,* whereas your sadism lay in your absolute indifference. It didn't matter to you one jot that a thousand people died when the ice cap shifted a few feet. You did not give a thought to the few odd thousand survivors on the hot side, the poor bums in the oven who managed to stay alive in a heat forty degrees above survival limit.

"They live like spaceship personnel, Grandon. They wash in undrinkable chemicals and every scrap of moisture has to be reclaimed; for a hundred and twenty years, they have lived on tears and sweat and urine. They try to roof their cities but hurricanes, laden with dust and continually blowing at speeds in excess of ninety miles an hour, produce a rate of erasure that is fantastic. Plastics and metals are ground away in a matter of months and the people have to go underground. There, even treble airlocks will not keep out the dust, and the people wear dust masks over their mouths and noses from birth to death. Forty-four percent of those people are doomed. They're suffering from a dust silicosis which will cut their life expectancy in half. You knew, Grandon, you knew and, no doubt, you were pleased by it. Your occupation was going according to plan."

He paused and sighed. "Think yourself damned lucky we are letting you go."

"I confess to being dubious of your assurances."

"No doubt. My personal reactions are to make you pay for the suffering you've caused, but if you return you will serve as a warning to the rest of your race. Believe me, before you leave, we are going to bleed you dry of any technical advantage you ever possessed, so that if your race tries reprisals they will be fighting their technical

139

equals. As you should know by now, we are an ingenious race and any weapons we take from you will be modified into something far worse. I warn you, Grandon, if your race comes into this sector of the galaxy again they will pay a price in destruction from which they will never recover."

Grandon did not answer; he knew it was true. In a straight fight, without the insidious weapons of exploitation and treachery, his race would never have taken the risk in the first place. What the humans called courage was, to him, suicidal aggression and his own race was not psychologically equipped to withstand it.

Liston placed a cigarette between his lips and lit it. "Now, about those shelters."

"Their erection would take years."

"Months. Your lives are at stake."

"If you let us go, we have only one ship."

"Don't start bargaining with me, Grandon. I hold all the cards. You will build your ships, if you wish to escape, in the same time you build the shelters. Incidentally, you will stock those shelters with food and necessities for five months beyond the estimated safety limit. You will make preparations at the same time for the floods, tempests and earthquakes of which you spoke."

"Mr. Liston, such a program is impossible."

"Don't make me laugh. You constructed the entire Co-temp zone in under ten years."

"With human help."

"True, but you now have over seven hundred of your own automatic factories to aid you, not to mention all the robot construction which has taken place over the last half-century."

"But Mr. Liston———"

"Save it. I'll give you six months; for every week beyond that period, one of your people will die."

Grandon moved hands and shoulders in a fluid helpless

gesture. He had tried for time, gambled on one last play and knew he had lost. His only hope of survival now was to obey.

Once the details were settled, response was immediate. Eighteen auto-factories were immediately retaped for the construction of various robotic units, the rest provided with a massive construction program of prefabricated building parts or synthetic foods.

Within a week, certain of the moving ways were cleared by order and used as conveyor belts to the construction areas in the neutral zone.

At the same time, work began on the construction of vast, impact-stressed hangars and on several alien space vessels. Construction was almost entirely robotic, but a team of scientists followed the work of the alien supervisors through from the beginning, asked endless questions and took copious notes. Liston was keeping his word about bleeding the aliens dry.

New-type robots began to appear on the streets; several huge buildings were demolished and huge trenches dug across the zone which later, when they began to reach out towards the ice cap, were widened and deepened to form canals.

Denning, inspecting them later, shook his head doubtfully. Were the aliens exaggerating or playing for time? Some of the canals were half a mile wide and went down to a depth of three thousand feet.

At the end of the fifteenth day, the first shelter was completed. It was a hundred feet tall, shaped like a beehive and constructed of curiously resilient plastic.

On the sixteenth day, two more shelters went up; on the seventeenth, five; on the eighteenth, nine. Thirty days later, as more and more parts became available and the number of robotic workers increased, shelter construction reached the incredible figure of four an hour.

When, two months later, output reached its maximum,

the figure reached eighteen an hour. The whole was under-taken by a veritable army of construction units, none of which resembled anything human and appeared to require no supervision.

Watching the tireless machines, Liston had inward doubts. Technically the aliens were miles ahead.

Dalkeith or one of his assistants kept him informed, however, with regular and comprehensive reports.

"It's not quite so damned clever as it looks," said Dalkeith dryly. "See that squat black building in the centre? That is the Program-Master, a kind of glorified computer. Each Program-Master is fed an instruction tape and given so much territory in which to work. All those cranes, hoists and multi-armed what-have-you's are not individual robots but extensions of the P-M. They respond to its broadcast impulses which, after all, only come from electronic symbols on the instruction tape."

"Could we do better?"

"Now we have the know-how, considerably. Technically these aliens are way ahead, but they lack our gift for im-provisation; they don't seem to exploit or explore like humans, and they lack our schoolboy enthusiasms."

Liston grinned faintly. "What the hell do you mean by that?"

Dalkeith laughed. "You know—let's put this stuff in a test tube, heat it and see what happens. They just lack the curiosity, or is it the nerve?"

"What's that construction over there?"

"Ah, that's my idea. I pointed out that we'd never move all the people out from under the ice with ground cars, at least, not in less than five years, so they're running up a moving way, right out to the glaciers."

Liston looked at him with respect. "Maybe you should have been a biogenetic."

"With due respects, sooner you than me."

142

"Well, thanks." Liston grinned and changed the subject. "Have you checked their original ship yet?"

"In detail."

"And their weapons?"

"They've only one, but it's a nasty one. It's a beam device which excites the atomic structure of any substance, including gas, with which it comes in contact, thus generating considerable heat. A ship, say in orbit, could burn a nasty little ring right around a planet, a ring about forty miles wide and ten feet deep."

Liston nodded, thoughtfully. "Well, you know what to do."

Dalkeith grinned wickedly. "Don't worry, old boy, I've done it."

Denning paced up and down his own private shelter, frequently glancing at his watch. "Superman," he thought bitterly. "Pity they hadn't included some more cold nerve in their creation." He was irritable, restless and unable to sit down.

It would have been better if there had been some company or, better still, if he had remained with Liston, but it had been decided that they should separate in case one of them perished in the coming unheaval.

He glanced again at his watch: six hours, five minutes. Had it stopped? He studied it, frowning. No, the second hand was still creeping round the dial; perhaps Earth watches didn't work so well on Firma.

Now that everything was so damned close, the restarting of axial rotation no longer seemed such a good idea. It did not seem possible either that so much had been accomplished in so short a time. In a few short months, not only had a secondary zone been constructed but several million people shifted into the safety area, regardless of their place of origin. Lollies shared shelters with Co-temps and

Buns, and rescue, administration and supply units were formed from all three.

The coexistence had not been accomplished without incident. There had been numerous fights and one murder.

Wherever possible, Z.P. units had been assigned to each shelter with strict orders to kill ruthlessly in the event of trouble. Unfortunately, there had not been enough policemen to go around, and here it had been necessary for Liston and Denning to appoint their own agents.

These agents had been assigned to particular trouble spots, and the results had been startling. The trouble-makers soon acquired a vast if terrified respect for curious-looking teenagers with a variety of miniature weapons dangling from their belts. Strangely, the pulsers had been unusually conscientious and quite impartial. If anyone, regardless of zone, made trouble, they chopped him. After a time, as *The Day* drew nearer, people began to understand that they were all in this together.

Denning glanced at his watch again. Only fifteen minutes. God! There *must* be something the matter with the damned thing.

If only he had received some news of Linda but, with all there had been to do, checking the millions of refugees had been impossible.

He switched on the viewer to pass the time and scowled. The unmoving sun was still partly bisected by one of the larger buildings in the Co-temp zone, the same dull, angry setting or rising sun which flung black shadows towards the cold. About him, the beehive shelters stretched away into endless distance and he wondered briefly if they would stand up to whatever was coming. He was a little vague as to what was coming, but he intended to watch it through the viewer.

Patrols were still moving about between the shelters, probably making sure that everything was secure. He noticed they were well wrapped up. Outside, even in this, the neutral zone, there were ten degrees of frost.

The admission panel lit, and he swore under his breath. Another blasted check. This was the third.

He touched the plate and the door slid silently back.

She didn't speak; she touched the plate closing the door behind her and came into his arms.

"Linda!" he said. "Linda. . . ."

Mark Liston was less fortunately placed. The burden of watching six alien scientists set out their equipment and restart the rotation of a planet was, he felt, too much for a woman. His ex-secretary was, therefore, very much against her will, in one of the safe buildings in the Co-temp zone.

"Seven minutes." The aliens seldom spoke now, and then only briefly.

"I know." Liston did not have to confirm the time; the seconds seemed to be ticking away in his head. Desperately, he tried to think. Was this the right thing to do? Was he gambling with millions of lives to fulfill a dream, a promise? Might not the repercussions be even worse than the aliens had suggested?

Had they thought of everything, or had everything been too damned easy? Was there any way in which the aliens could effect some treachery in the last few minutes?

He frowned worriedly at the equipment. The device didn't look as if it could shift a planet on its axis; in point of fact, it didn't look as if it could shift itself, let alone anything else.

He had imagined a huge room filled with complex devices and vibrating with power but this—Was this the treachery, a gigantic hoax before the aliens struck back?

The alien device was a blank, black cube about a foot high and three feet long. Standing erect at each corner was a short rod terminating in a colorless transparent prism about the size of a walnut. There was nothing more, no dials, no switches and no wires or source of power.

"It looks," he thought savagely, "like a small coffin with nobs on. God, I'm being conned, I'm being sold a gold brick—or a black one—and I've given them a blank check against countless human lives for it."

"Eight seconds."

One of the prisms lit, flickered, then slowly turned to an angry and sullen green.

"Four seconds."

Two more prisms lit, turned green, and finally the fourth.

"Zero!"

Outside, the sky seemed to split. A streak of lightning zigzagged across and vanished beyond the horizon.

Seconds later, thunder rolled, muffled and echoing like the dull rumble of a distant war.

Silence. Nothing seemed to happen. The aliens stared at their device and Liston licked his lips and wished he had someone to talk to. How long would this go on?

It went on for thirty minutes, but it was a tense thirty minutes. Men absently touching their hair were startled to see sparks. There was a dry smell of ozone and a sense of oppression.

At the end of thirty minutes, those watching saw the sun apparently vanish and reappear and, although they did not hear it, they had the feeling that the entire planet groaned protestingly.

The planet did groan, groaned and shuddered.

On the cold side, a glacier shifted seventy feet. The glacier was thirty-seven miles long and a thousand feet thick. Already poised on the lip of a precipice, the avalanche shook the ground for three hundred miles and the echoes of its impact continued for nearly five minutes.

Relatively, however, it was a small and almost apologetic overture to what was to follow.

Ten minutes later, there was an earth tremor and a fissure opened in the earth. The fissure, following geographical weakness, was six hundred and eight miles in length and half a mile wide. It ran, jagged as a streak of lightning, right across the neutral area and deep into the temperate zone.

Then it closed in a geyser of debris with the savage finality of a sprung trap.

The impact of its closing flung people to the floor and, in the immediate area, the shelters danced and jumped like toys.

Shaken rescue squads emerged to render what aid they could, but there was not much they could do. Forty-seven shelters had completely disappeared and, one, only partly engulfed, had been crushed to the thickness of matchboard.

In the temperate zone, six of the great buildings had also disappeared and two, like displaced pyramids, had been flung on their sides. One had a gigantic hole in its side.

More important, however, the area rescue squad had vanished with one of the buildings, and from the damaged building came the screams of injured and frightened children.

In Building Eight, which had escaped direct damage, Jessina Pallis stared from the window and rubbed her eyes. Jessina was thirty with a beautiful but ravaged face.

"Children crying." Her eyes misted. It was real, wasn't it?

Jessina had devoted her teens to a succession of lovers and her twenties to similar excesses but in the perfection of dream-drugs.

"Children crying," she said, again. "They're real kids, aren't they? I didn't specify a dream like this."

"Lolly kids," said a harsh voice.

"Children—they're hurt." Unaccountably there were

147

tears in her eyes. "I can't stand it—can't stand hearing them cry like that."

"Turn the sound off, then."

"No, no, it won't make any difference. I shall still go on hearing it in my mind—I'm going out there."

The building shook again to another tremor.

"You're mad, you'll be killed—stop her, someone."

"Stop her yourself—I'm going with her. I can't stand it either."

Within minutes, over seventy Co-temp women had taken the place of the rescue squads in rescuing Lolly children. Humanity was learning to live together again.

On the hot side, the mother and father of all tornadoes had built up—a screaming funnel of blackness, gouging a trench a hundred and fifty feet wide and eighteen feet deep. Rocks as big as two-story buildings were snatched up and hurled into the sky before it finally struck the wind barriers and went shrieking away into the deserts again. The zone was bombarded with huge rocks for several seconds.

Chapter Fifteen

Again the sun vanished and reappeared and, on the hot side, four hundred square miles of desert began to shiver and flow like water. Then the entire area dropped ninety feet and did not rise again.

As if to compensate, nine hundred miles to the east, six miles of black and jagged rock rose suddenly from the bed of the desert to the height of two hundred feet, forming a small and sharply defined mountain range.

The entire surface of the planet shifted and crumpled protestingly. Six more earthquakes shook the neutral zone, and eight more shelters were completely destroyed.

On the cold side, another fissure opened in the earth and this one reached down to the planet's fiery core, already shifting from unimaginable pressures. Fire, incandescent gases and molten rock—converted by pressure and heat to the fluidity of water—rushed upwards through the vent and found itself tamped down by five thousand feet of solid ice.

Beneath the surface, the ice was converted instantly to superheated steam, and a pressure head built up such as had never been conceived in all history. Something had to give and the resultant explosion made the first atomic device look like a puff of smoke.

Four hundred square miles of ice simply ceased to exist or was hurled upwards in the column of flame, smoke and debris which spurted twelve thousand feet into the sky.

A vast mushroom cloud began to spread out over the stars and, in the immediate area of the newly formed crater, a thick and blinding fog, lit bloodily from the sea flame, began to roll across the glaciers.

The thunder of the explosion reached the neutral area several seconds after the impact of the eruption had been felt through the soles of the feet.

Linda clung desperately to Denning. "What was it—I'm frightened."

Denning stroked her hair gently. "I don't know—and so am I." He tried to make the remark sound amused and casual but had the uncomfortable feeling that his voice had quivered uncertainly.

A few miles away, Liston, strapped in a safety chair, had his gun pointed. "Does it have to be this rough?"

The aliens made faint disparaging movements with their hands. "It is as you chose. Had we restored rotation in our own time, in our own way, the task would have taken twelve years, but the repercussions would have been far less violent." Then, as if to rub salt into the wound, they added, "Irrespective of your impatience, axial rotation has begun; to brake that rotation now would disintegrate the crust and thus completely destroy the planet. . . ."

Two hours later, apart from continual and violent earth tremors, observers saw the backwash of the eruption.

Winds increased to hurricane force and the hurricanes brought both hail and blizzards. Snow carried horizontally by the shrieking winds soon obscured shelter from shelter, but it was a snow such as man had never seen before. A snow heavy with fragments of volcanic dust and minute shards of pumice—black snow.

The hail which followed, including chunks of ice, was also black and often half pumice; some of the hailstones were as big as a man's head.

In one of the shelters, however, a group of scientists were checking with the equipment which had survived the earth tremors.

"She's *moving!*"

"You're sure?"

"Check for yourself. It's a labored crawl, but it's movement."

Twenty-four hours later, the sky cleared and the change was discernible in the Co-temp zone but had moved appreciably above them.

Twenty-four hours later, however, relatively and visually, the sun had only risen a foot from its original position and, twenty-four hours after that, only two feet.

The effect of the change, however, was clearly visible in the neutral zone. The temperature was now well above freezing point and the iron-hard ground had become a sea of mud.

Near the limits of the glaciers, the temperatures had risen from minus eighteen to minus six.

Forty-eight hours later, the mud and water in the neutral zone were drying rapidly. The temperature was like that of a warm spring day.

Near the glaciers, however, there was a new and curiously unfamiliar sound—the steady drip of water. The temperature had risen a degree above freezing.

Five days later, the drip had turned to the roar of countless cascades. The barren ground had turned to an inland sea which groaned with ice.

Ten days later, the sun was at its zenith above the ice cap and the atmospheric temperature had soared from twenty-two below to twenty-five above.

An enormous pall of fog blanketed the entire area, but beneath it the noise was absolute and continuous: a racing of waters, the continual thunder of avalanches, the rending and crashing of ice.

Cloud masses drifted away to the hot side which, after many hours of darkness, had lost its heat, and there the cloud masses froze and drifted downwards to the sand.

Within twelve hours the deserts had a four-inch blanket of snow.

The effects of the unnatural thaw were soon seen and felt in the neutral zone. Water began to trickle along the beds of the immensely deep canals; the trickle became a stream and the stream a raging torrent which rose rapidly.

Worse, the water was thick with huge fragments of ice which increased in size as the days passed, and soon the canals were jammed solid. Heroic attempts by volunteers to blast the jams met with only temporary success; soon the canals were jammed solid again.

The water rose above the banks and in many places the floods were seventy feet deep.

Fortunately, the shelters were loosely anchored and designed to float, but the real hazard came from the ice—great drifting cliffs, in some cases as big as three-story buildings.

A large number of shelters were holed or ground between huge packs, and once again the half-trained, ill-equipped and inexperienced rescue squads did their best with ground cars from the central rescue pool.

A ground car with its cushion of energy could ride just as successfully on water as on dry land, but the rescuers were badly inexperienced and, although individually heroic, poorly directed.

Paulus Kostain, watching through a viewer, found himself clenching and unclenching his hands. "To leeward, you fools, not *that* side—God, they'll lose more lives than they can save!"

Eighteen more distress calls came in from other damaged shelters, and it occurred to Kostain suddenly that he had never been officially relieved of his post. What those teams needed was not only support but coordination and direction.

On an impulse he banged the general police switch.

"Attention, Guardian Service and S.M.3, this is an emergency, repeat, emergency——"

It was a tribute to Kostain's personality and Service image that he got a sixty percent response.

Within an hour his private ground car arrived at the shelter, and two hours later he was directing a local rescue operation and, at the same time, coordinating several more through the medium of the viewer screens.

"Tovin, take over the direction of Number Twenty-Seven for a minute or so. Number Eighteen has run into pack ice."

A huge cliff of ice bore down on him suddenly and he slid the car skilfully out of the way.

"Tovin? Come in, Tovin——"

There was no response and, frowning, Kostain switched on the search unit.

Exactly forty seconds later he found it. Tovin's ground car was already two miles away and racing over the ice-packed muddy waters to the comparative safety of the Co-temp zone.

Kostain did not ask himself what Tovin was doing—he knew. Tovin had lost his nerve and was running. He was running for one of the great buildings, one of the women's blocks and there, once safe, he would amuse himself.

Kostain reached forward and touched a switch. Cross hairs appeared in the search screen, firing coordinates.

Kostain touched a stud. Two miles away, the water boiled upwards in a white column of steam and in its center Tovin's ground car turned abruptly cherry red, crumpled and vanished from sight. A few oily bubbles appeared on the surface, a wisp of smoke, then nothing.

Kostain turned back to his instruments. "Number Ten, close up to position two, Number Six——"

At the end of twenty-four hours, the rescue squads under Kostain's direction had successfully saved more than four thousand people.

As the days passed, the floods began slowly to subside. The water had found new channels for itself, which the ice had gouged wider, and several of the stoppages in the canals had collapsed under the enormous pressure of water.

Then, for the first time in a hundred and twenty years, darkness fell on the hot side.

The first complete revolution of the planet took forty-seven days.

The second, thirty-five days.

The third, twenty days.

One hundred and ninety days from the first movement, axial rotation had returned to its normal twenty-four hours.

By this time, enormous rivers were rolling into the deserts in muddy torrents, pushing the sands before them and beginning to fill the salt beds of forgotten oceans. Already there were huge swirling lakes, islands and, here and there, the dim imprint of half-remembered shore-lines.

The planet was still shaken with frequent earth tremors and gigantic thunder storms swept its surface, but there was night and day and the first hint of the coming of seasons.

Fourteen huge and extremely active volcanic craters belched smoke into the sky from various parts of the surface, deluging the surrounding terrain with lava, pumice and volcanic ash.

It was like awakening and, again, it was like rebirth.

Reports began to come in.

One hundred and fifty thousand people had perished in the upheaval; two hundred thousand had been seriously injured.

Veigler, under shelter arrest, stormed at his guards. "I warned them—lives cast needlessly away."

One of the guards scowled at him. "According to the records, six and a half million died when rotation stopped, another fifteen million in the four years which followed. To my mind, we've come through it damned lightly."

"Those figures are pure propaganda."

The guard, after several months in Veigler's company, was completely disenchanted. He said, "Ah shaddup," rudely.

Two hundred and seventy-five days after re-revolution, humanity emerged from the shelters and, one hundred and ten days after that, a number of them gathered together on a long narrow island which had formed on what had been the hot side.

It was late afternoon. The sky was clear, but huge cloud masses reared themselves in the east.

Humanity had named the island in advance. They called it "Departure Isle."

With the humans were nearly two hundred aliens, true aliens, divested of human clothing and their human synthetic faces—a line of black faceless ant-things guarded by grim-looking men with a variety of weapons.

Remote control devices activated circuits miles away and great doors slid open. Huge black vessels rose from their stressed cocoons beneath the earth.

Slowly, like huge bulbous dirigibles, they began to float under radio control towards the island.

They were brought down in a rough arc, and the alien prisoners were formed into a single line in preparation for departure.

One by one, almost ceremoniously, the chains with their lethal lockets were removed and the aliens filed into the waiting ships.

One hour later, in the gathering dusk the great ships rose and began to lift towards the sky. Slowly they seemed to dwindle in size, became the size of eggs, then black specks and, finally, nothing.

There was no sigh, no cheer. The watchers turned and began to pack up their equipment. Loaded ground cars began to leave the island, sliding over the water toward the mainland.

Only a small group remained. Liston, Denning, Linda and a few others.

Liston put his arm round his ex-secretary. "So far, so good."

"Perhaps too good to be true," said a quiet voice behind him.

Liston turned. "What the hell are you doing here?"

"A good question." Kostain smiled tiredly. "I am surrendering myself with, I confess, some misgiving, but voluntarily."

"Conscience?"

"Mr. Liston, you flatter me. This is purely character weakness. I am not the stuff of which fugitives are made. I prefer to give myself up now rather than endure the doubtful privileges of a free quarry."

Liston frowned at him. "You did a first-class job of rescue work. Several thousand people owe you their lives."

"Several hundred don't," said Kostain, drily.

"Nonetheless, you have courage and administrative ability. Firma could use a man of your qualifications." He looked at the other thoughtfully. "Divested of that rather flashy uniform, I doubt very much if I should recognize you again. Incidentally, if you apply for a position anywhere I suggest you avoid police work."

"Thank you." Kostain saluted. It was clear for the first time in his life he was moved to respect.

"Oh, before you go—what did you mean about it being too good to be true?"

Kostain shrugged faintly. "It is. I know these creatures. If nothing else, they are tenacious. Oh, yes, I know their position became precarious, particularly with the introduction of your—er—necklaces but, even so, it seems to me they gave in too easily. In the long run, psychologically, they should have found an answer. In the long run, they should have outwitted you. The way they caved in at the end is a complete reverse of their normal psychology and, frankly, I am suspicious."

Liston smiled a little wearily. "The reason they 'caved in,' as you put it, was that, as I explained to them, *in the long run they couldn't win.*"

Kostain blinked at him. "I'm afraid I don't understand you."

"It's simple enough when understood. Our original bio-genetic creators planned for three phases which, they hoped, would take care of everything. Phase one was adaption whereby we could live without scientific aid on any part of the planet, regardless of conditions. Phase two was aggressive; a physical superiority, a built-in antipathy to all things alien and the hypersensitive faculties for recognizing them, irrespective of appearance or disguise.

"Phase three, however, was the real stroke of genius— *the ability to procreate our kind.* The planners made damned sure we would, too. They trebled our sexual urges and rearranged our hormones so that we became irresistibly attractive to the opposite sex."

Liston paused and lit a cigarette. "When you informed me before deportation that I was responsible for at least twenty pregnancies, let me assure you, without pride, you'd missed at least thirty and there may have been more. In ten years or so, there would have been thirty or so teenage super beings out hunting; a few years more and there would be double that number. Already, the aliens had been seriously embarrassed by just two. It was clear, even to them, that within a century they would be completely overwhelmed. You see, Kostain, they knew that in the long run they were bound to lose."

Liston exhaled smoke and laughed shortly. "I must confess I rubbed salt into the wound. I pointed out that it was

157

a little too late to play Herod and run around killing all the first born and, in any case, *which* first born——"

"Now!" said Denning, who had not ceased to stare at the sky.

They followed his gaze. It was now almost evening. The sky was almost dark and stars were appearing. To the east, however, above the black shoulders of the cloud bank, new stars were appearing—a group of stars which increased in size and brilliance as they watched and seemed suddenly to erupt.

The flash lit the sky from horizon to horizon and turned the clouds to a shimmering unnatural blue. Then it faded, leaving only a few streaks of phosphorescent blue which rapidly faded.

Liston sighed. "If you've never seen a reactor unit become critical, you've seen one now."

Kostain frowned slightly. "A settlement, and a proper one, but I must confess you surprise me, Mr. Liston. I thought you lacked the realism to serve them with their own coins."

Liston shook his head. "I didn't; they served themselves. When one is dealing with a culture to whom the word 'gratitude' is an abstraction and betrayal an accepted weapon, one must make preparations. The aliens had one dangerous weapon with which they could have turned this planet to a cinder. We therefore rigged that weapon, prior to their departure, so that, should it be employed, it would kick back into their drive motors. If they had been psychologically capable of leaving it alone and not bent on dealing the last card, they would have escaped to safety——"

They walked slowly in ones and twos back to the shoreline.

"No," Liston was saying. "There will have to be democratic elections. Wisely we were not created for dictator material——"

Linda pressed close to Denning. "I wish it were light. I saw it as we landed and wanted to point it out to you then, but you were too busy."

"Point out what?"

"This used to be desert on the hot side. As we landed, I saw tiny green shoots near that rock—the first blades of grass in a hundred and twenty years."

His arms tightened about her. "And if you imagine I have the patience to hang around here until someone builds us another haystack, you're very much mistaken."